THE PRINCE OF CENTRAL PARK

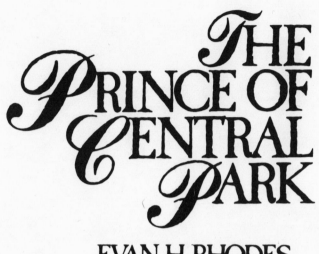

THE PRINCE OF CENTRAL PARK

EVAN H. RHODES

COWARD, McCANN & GEOGHEGAN, INC.
NEW YORK

SBN: 698-10643-1
Library of Congress Catalog Card Number: 74-16650

PRINTED IN THE UNITED STATES OF AMERICA

For Dick Duane

PART ONE

One

"**S**top, thief! Catch him! Thief!"

Running like he'd never run before, Jay-jay fled before his pursuers. His shins ached with each jarring step, and his breath seared in his lungs. Ahead of him, the alarmed Saturday afternoon strollers scattered. Two ladies wheeling baby carriages took up the cry; an old man waved his cane over his head and joined the chase after the eleven-year-old boy.

Jay-jay gasped for breath. Don't look back! he thought desperately, feeling the storekeeper gaining on him. If I can reach Central Park, once I'm in the park—

The tenements along Cathedral Parkway rushed past Jay-jay, shimmering in his fogged glasses. Just as he reached the corner of Central Park West the traffic light changed. Without a second thought Jay-jay raced across the avenue.

Brakes screeched, cars swerved as he dodged the oncoming motorists, and the air resounded with blaring horns and the curses of snarled traffic.

For a fleeting instant Jay-jay thought, Maybe somebody's watching today? Otherwise, I'd have been run over for sure.

The boy gained the 110th Street entrance of the park and dashed through the Stranger's Gate. Blocked by the flow of traffic, the storekeeper stood on the opposite corner, ranting and shaking his fist.

"It's not the peach," he cried, buttonholing the people in the crowd. "But every day—and twice this month they broke in—and they raised the rent—"

On and on Jay-jay ran, the massed green of the park drawing him swiftly to itself. Down a waterfall of stone steps he leapt, five and nine and eleven and nine again, down deeper into the cool safety of silver birch and weeping forsythia and winding pathways.

His side began to ache with a spasmodic pain and he was forced to slow to a jog. The path separated; to the left it curved through a cavernous tunnel and surfaced onto a flat stretch of meadow where there were picnicking people and children in playgrounds and ultimately the naked, unprotected waters of the Harlem Meer.

"Not that way," Jay-jay warned himself, heaving for breath. "If they corner me there they'll catch me easy."

To the right, the path dipped and snaked into the wild jungle part of the park. Reaching for the sun, sycamore, elm and poplar cast deep shadows over the terrain. Ahead lay the dangerous territory of the Cliff and the

Blockhouse. There, Jay-jay knew, bands of teenagers roamed over the treacherous cliffs and stalked the dense forest. Ready to rip off any unsuspecting passersby who'd wandered into their hunting grounds. Or if there wasn't any better prey, then the stronger muggers mugged the weaker muggers.

Never before had Jay-jay dared venture into this wilderness. He wiped the sweat from his nose and adjusted his eyeglasses. At eleven, he was slightly undersized, greatly undernourished, and rarely a match for the kids in his class.

"Let alone for a whole gang of older guys," he muttered.

But the alternative was worse. If he got caught—never mind the storekeeper. The cops would take him back home where Ardis would be waiting, ready to beat him black and blue for what he'd done.

"I'll just have to take my chances," Jay-jay said, and swung right. His jog slowed as he left the path and cut into a tangle of rhododendron, hawthorn and spined barberry. The ground buckled and thrust with massive outcroppings of mica-glinting granite.

Jay-jay caught a glimpse of a trail winding up to the Blockhouse. His eyes traveled to the crest of the Cliff. Outlined against the sky he saw a distant figure. A guy. On the lookout for an adventure in the bushes? Jay-jay wondered. Or a scout for one of the gangs. Jay-jay didn't wait to find out. He veered away and headed south toward the Great Hill.

A brilliant patch of green where the groundwater broke through to the surface. Here, the boulders were covered with moss; rock slabs were precariously balanced, and he hopped from one to the other as he made his way. Back on to the path again. Up steps now, nine and then seven. Here, weeds had broken the asphalt of the footpaths. Here, along the less traveled roads there was no trail of garbage left by people.

Jay-jay sensed that the immediate danger of the chase was past but he couldn't help himself. Like some hunted thing running from his past he drove himself on.

His stomach rumbled and he kneaded it to ease the pangs. "If only I'd managed to hold onto that peach," he said, shaking his head. But he'd dropped it the minute the storekeeper had spotted him.

Jay-jay hadn't had anything to eat in about twenty-four hours. Or to drink. But he couldn't go home. Not after what he'd done. Ever.

With that memory, Jay-jay's head began to reel. His legs buckled and he sank to his knees. Jay-jay grabbed tufts of razor grass to keep the ground from turning, faster and faster it spun until it ripped free from his grasp and swung up to crack him in the head, shattering his eyeglasses.

Jay-jay pitched forward into the dark world of the apartment-hotel, into the looming presence of Ardis, falling and falling back into the nightmare from which he'd run.

Two

Everything happened because there was no school. On the first Monday after Labor Day, PS 145 had opened. By Tuesday it was shut down tight. Something about a fight over community control. Which had led to a teachers' strike. Which had led to a parent boycott. Which meant that all day long, for three solid weeks, Jay-jay had no place to go.

From the moment Jay-jay had come to live with this foster mother, two months ago, Ardis had made it plain, with some choice slaps, that she didn't want him home before dark.

When Jay-jay asked her "How come?" Ardis snapped, "Never you mind, I got my reasons."

It was on Friday, the day before he fled into the park that it all came to a boil.

Most of Jay-jay's morning was taken up with cleaning

the empty lot across from the church. The Block Association had started the project in high gear. But Jay-jay was pretty discouraged when everybody quit after a couple of hours, leaving him a lone figure in the junk-strewn mess. His labors weren't a total loss because he found a threadbare tire, rolled it to the gas station, and sold it for a quarter.

A nickel bought a box of colored chalk. But right in the middle of drawing his sidewalk mural—a laser-beam battle between the space ships of *Star Trek* and *The Starlost*, the janitor of the building came after Jay-jay with a broom.

Later that afternoon, Jay-jay wandered over to the schoolyard and tried to shoot some lay-ups with a bunch of older white and Puerto Rican guys. What with his eyeglasses slipping and some big dude elbowing him, Jay-jay was getting the worst of it until Officer Blutkopf, the school security guard, herded them out of the playground. Closing time.

Jay-jay moped around . Then his heart sprang up when he spotted Dolores, the prettiest girl in his class, sitting on the steps of the pool hall. Though it was a major investment, Jay-jay decided it was worth it and he blew a dime on a twin Popsicle. But just as soon as Dolores had finished eating her half, she abandoned Jay-jay to play Ping-Pong with a senior in junior high. Leaving Jay-jay with a broken heart that would never mend.

He kicked-the-can all around the block, plotting intricate tortures for all junior high seniors. Then he pondered the important question, What to do next?

"You could always walk over to the park," he told himself.

Jay-jay dug Central Park, it was the one place that had

made these months with Ardis bearable. In fact, at the beginning of summer, Jay-jay had picked up a free map of the park at the playground near the Warrior's Gate. Wandering about, he got to know the peaceful area around the Harlem Meer pretty well, but the wild reaches of the Great Hill, the Cliff and the Blockhouse, and all the unknown territory below Ninety-seventh Street, all of these were mysteries that begged to be explored.

"But not now," Jay-jay said with a glance at the setting sun. It would be twilight soon and everybody knew that the park was way too dangerous after dark.

So Jay-jay had drifted home. "A little too early, maybe," he warned himself. But he'd run out of things to do, there were no kids left in the streets, and he was hungry.

He began the long climb up the eight flights to the apartment, shivering as he passed each gloomy landing. But "climbing the stairs" odds were way better than "riding the elevator" odds. The first rule of survival in the apartment house: Never Take the Elevator If You're Alone.

As Jay-jay passed the third floor landing, a bag of garbage whizzed by. Up he climbed, nose crinkling against the smell of dead rats and pee. It hadn't taken Jay-jay long to know the building. The fights, the laughter, the screams of the hippie couple on a bad trip. The daily dealings in the hallways, kids looking to score from their pushers. And every day the kids got younger and younger.

"Here man, try some of this," a snappy dude with a mustache had said one day to Jay-jay. "Make you feel high and happy."

But luckily, Jay-jay had just watched a scene like that on a *Mod Squad* rerun, and he'd beat it, fast.

Sex was everywhere, behind the closed doors of the sharp pimps and their high-stepping chicks; up on the roof landing; the German wino-lady on the ninth floor who wondered what kind of a kick it would be to ball an eleven-year-old.

But Jay-jay wasn't ready for love; his body wasn't quite there. Besides, he didn't trust anybody.

"I wish I had a million dollars so I could get out of this place," Jay-jay muttered, hopping over a mop and a pail. "I'll go to Alaska. Or I'll find the source of the Amazon and name it after me, or I'll discover Atlantis, or—"

Seventh, eighth floor, and at last Jay-jay reached the flat. He pressed his ear against the door, heard the television set and figured the coast was clear. And walked into a tableau of two half-naked, scrambling people.

Screaming above the canned laughter of *The Price Is Right!*, Ardis shouted for him to "Get the hell out of here!"

Jay-jay ducked an ashtray and scooted out the door. About to start down the steps, Jay-jay caught a glimpse of the wino-lady walking up the stairwell toward him.

"I'll never get past without her grabbing me," he breathed.

In his confusion, Jay-jay forgot the first rule of survival. He pressed the elevator button and it creaked up to the eighth floor. Jay-jay got in. Pressed lobby. The car started down and jerked to a halt on five. A guy with a face right out of *Weird Comics* bounded through the door, jamming his foot against the gate to keep the elevator from moving.

In that instant, Jay-jay knew. He tried to charge out of the elevator, but the guy grabbed his arm and slammed him against the wall.

"Empty your pockets," the voice said.

Jay-jay stared at the apparition. Nose, eyes and mouth were melted together by the nylon stocking pulled over the guy's head. Even with that, Jay-jay thought he recognized him by the way he kept hunching his shoulders, and by the bluish needle tracks on his wiry white arms.

Elmo, the neighborhood rip-off artist. Sixteen, maybe seventeen, hooked on the galloping white horse. Elmo didn't have enough smarts to pull off any of the big jobs. And he wasn't strong enough yet to take on the shopkeepers. Old ladies and kids were his special meat.

"Come on, hand it over," Elmo hissed.

Jay-jay aimed a kung fu kick at Elmo's shin. The switchblade was at Jay-jay's throat before he could make another move.

Don't fight back, screamed the warning siren in Jay-jay's head. This guy's so far out of it he'll knife you in a second. With a deep anger that that karate kick only seemed to work on television, Jay-jay handed it over.

"Fifteen cents?" Elmo said, squinting through the nylon stocking. "Where are you hiding the rest of it?"

In short order, Elmo had stripped Jay-jay down to his underwear, stuffing clothes, his Japanese rubber sandals, and the fifteen cents into an airline bag.

"The medal too," came the muffled voice as Elmo spotted the medallion hanging around Jay-jay's neck.

Jay-jay backed against the elevator wall. He had only the dimmest memory of his mother, but the orphanage had told him the medal had been hers. It was a flat medallion with Mary in bas-relief offering her child to the world.

"No, please," Jay-jay said. "See? It isn't gold or anything. It even makes my skin turn green."

But Elmo's eyes stayed riveted on the medallion. His hand moved reflexively to his pants pocket and closed around a long rawhide thong. Tied to the thong were odd pieces of cheap jewelry: a ring, the charm off a bracelet, a key, a cigarette lighter. Every time Elmo mugged somebody he kept a memento of the rip-off, as though that special totem gave him all the powers of his victim. In a way, it was like collecting scalps, for each conquest made Elmo feel that he was better, more powerful, more important than the person he'd conquered. And in the low pecking order of his life, it was a feeling that Elmo needed desperately in order to survive.

If only I can kick his foot away from the gate, get the elevator moving, maybe somebody—Jay-jay's mind raced.

Elmo reached for the medallion and Jay-jay knocked his hand away. The knifepoint dug into Jay-jay's neck, drawing a dot of blood. Jay-jay winced and tried to duck under but Elmo grabbed the chain and yanked it over Jay-jay's head. Then he shoved Jay-jay out of the elevator, knocking him to the floor.

"One word out of you and I'll—" the switchblade made a menacing slash in the air. Elmo's fingers closed around the medal. This one was important, because the kid had fought back.

Elmo released the gate and the elevator doors slid shut. Jay-jay watched the indicator jerk down, four, three, two. The car reached the lobby before Jay-jay managed to get himself together. Scrambling to his feet, he darted up the steps to the apartment. Jay-jay didn't care about anything else, only the medal.

Crying and kicking, he pounded on the door. Wouldn't Ardis ever come? The door swung open suddenly and Jay-jay tumbled in. Ardis, still in her underwear, took one look at the boy shivering in his underwear and shouted, "What happened?" Then it dawned on her.

She threw her hands up in the air. "You took the elevator, didn't you?" she yelled, and cracked him across the face. "How many times do I have to tell you? You're not worth the trouble! Not for that stinking support check. Why do I always wind up with the dumb ones? Why me? I just bought you new clothes and shoes and—"

The next minutes were bedlam. Jay-jay yelling for her to call the cops, the hulking boyfriend yanking his clothes on—"Cops? Can't get involved. Jesus! My job and—" and Ardis alternately trying to placate her man and swatting at the boy, and the squeals of the newlyweds on the twenty-five inch color TV who'd just won a mink coat and a mobile home and a chromium-plated garbage dispos-all.

A couple of hours later, Jay-jay sat hunkered on his cot in the living room. Ardis bustled in and out of the bathroom putting on her makeup for the big weekend.

"Good thing it's Friday," she told her wide blue eyes in the mirror as she glued on false eyelashes. Good thing the bar would be jumping. Good thing her man had promised to meet her there.

"Good thing for you," she said, taking a swipe at

Jay-jay's head as she passed through. "Now stop sniffling, hear? I didn't hit you that hard."

Jay-jay's fingers moved aimlessly at the empty place around his neck.

Ardis hadn't hit him anyplace where it would show. Black and blue marks showed up on this thin-skinned kid like neon lights. That pissy-eyed social worker—a few days before she came on her visit, Ardis made damned sure the apartment was clean and that she'd been extra nice to the kid. Anyway, Miss Bleeding Heart wouldn't be around again for three, maybe four months. And then, reminded that she'd have to buy Jay-jay a whole new outfit, Ardis gave him another good crack.

"Damn! I counted on that money. The payment on the TV's coming up."

Ardis was not a mean woman. In a world of rip-offs she saw nothing wrong with her own brand. She'd been exploited dumb and blind when she'd worked as a single-needle operator in her youth. And as for moral decay? Hell! She'd paid more in income taxes than Tricky had on a half a million dollars, so who were they to talk about moral decay?

Then Ardis had chanced on the foster mother ploy. Somebody to fetch and carry, help her clean, most of all, listen to her complaints. She did give the kids a home. None of them had ever starved. So what if she was a little free with her hands sometimes? Hadn't her parents been that way with her?

"And didn't I turn out all right? she asked, coming back into the living room on a wave of Jungle Passion perfume. "Leave that Band-Aid alone," she said, slapping his hand away from his neck. "No watching TV all night. You got the radio. I don't want you buining it

out the very first month I bought it, hear?'' Her eyes
narrowed. "I'll be home early tonight, and if I catch
you—I got special secret ways of finding out if you used
it.''

Her whole rap was a lie, Jay-jay knew. She never
came home early. Special secret ways? She couldn't
even empty the vacuum cleaner, let alone have special
secret ways. He hated this TV; at least she'd let him
watch the old black and white set.

"There's peanut butter in the cabinet and milk and a
Twinkie for dessert, though you don't deserve it. See if
you can't stay out of trouble for once in your life, hear?''

The blond one tonight, Ardis decided and slipped the
curly wig over her lank brown hair. Blonds had more
fun, they said, and after the interruption this afternoon
she needed a *lot* of fun. She splashed some more Jungle
Passion on the inside of her thighs, stuffed some bills
deep in her cleavage, strapped on her platform shoes and
teetered out the door for the big night.

Jay-jay listened to the shoes clack in the hallway. He
reached for the TV set but stopped short. Something was
wrong. What? Then he realized that the sound of her
footsteps hadn't receded. She's walking in place! Jay-jay
scrambled back onto the cot just as Ardis burst back into
the apartment, her eyes darting to the set. She seemed
disappointed not to find it on.

The scarlet-tipped finger poked at him. "I'm warning
you,'' and then she bent down absently, gave him a kiss
and was gone.

This time Jay-jay watched from the window until he
saw Ardis' foreshortened figure leaving the building.
Then he undressed, tried to do a few head stands, fell
over mostly, and finally turned on the set.

A show about a family of kids singing their hearts out and becoming rock and roll stars. Then *The Movie of the Week*, some fairy tale about an honest cop. The ball game. Then *One Step Beyond*, about a one-eyed gypsy who forecast her own murder.

"I ain't scared of that," Jay-jay said, switching fast to another channel.

On the *Eleventh Hour News*, the anchor man told Jay-jay that his school strike had been settled. "Barring any major disagreements, classes will start on Monday."

"What a relief," Jay-jay yawned to the announcer.

Bad as school could be, and it could be bad, at least it was someplace to go.

Then another piece of news from the almost disbelieving broadcaster. "The Food and Drug Administration has just confirmed that one third of all the dog food sold in the United States is used for human consumption."

"Tell us something new," Jay-jay said to the commentator, remembering Tuesday night. But he had to give Ardis points there, because whenever she put it on the table, she ate it too. Anyway, it wasn't *so* bad, provided you heated it real good and you didn't look at the picture of the dog on the can.

The stock market was down, inflation was up, Russia, China, and America were at each other's throats again for some reason, the Mets lost, tomorrow's weather, hazy. Air quality: Unacceptable.

Then *The Late Show*. Just before a lot of pretty movie stars won the old west from renegade Indians, Jay-jay dozed off.

Into a beautiful dream, about a restaurant that served a hundred different kinds of spaghetti: with meat balls, with clam sauce, with garlic and butter, with chocolate ice cream. He'd ordered a plate of each and was about to dig in—

A hand yanked him up from the cot and out of his sleep. Jay-jay opened his eyes to a kaleidoscope of reds, greens, and blues and heard a crackle and a buzzing in his ears.

"I warned you!" Ardis cried, and began shaking him until Jay-jay thought his head would snap off. "Now you've gone and done it," she slurred. "Burned out the picture tube! Feel it!" she said, slapping the top of the set. "It's burning hot!"

"I didn't do anything, I—" Jay-jay tried to explain that the set wasn't broken, the network had just stopped transmitting for the night, but Ardis was too drunk to listen.

Ardis shoved him back on the cot and the canvas creaked under his fall. Frantically, she turned the knob back and forth, but each new click of the channel selector only brought louder buzzing and a fuzzier screen.

Jay-jay crouched against the wall, trying like crazy to think of a way out of this one. She was drunk, drunker than he'd ever seen her. It happened maybe once every three weeks. She'd go off on a tear, come back from the neighborhood gin mill, crash around the apartment, beat up on him a little and then pass out.

Jay-jay started to edge off the cot when Ardis screamed hoarsely. The tuning knob had come off in her hand. "See what you did?" she cried, her eyes filling with tears of frustration.

Jay-jay crossed his arms over his head to protect himself from the rain of blows.

"Nothing ever goes right for me," Ardis sobbed. "Why me? A brand-new set and you—that son-of-a-bitch never showed up! And that guy I bought two drinks? The nerve! To waltz off with that trampy barmaid! I wouldn't have had to go out tonight if *you* hadn't come home early! And *you* had to get yourself mugged naked! And *you*—"

The complaints blubbered from her slack lips. Jay-jay didn't even try to answer. No matter what he said, he knew it would wind up being his fault. Everything that went wrong around here was his fault. Somehow, that seemed to make Ardis' life more bearable.

"Don't you hit me! Don't you dare!" Ardis yelled as Jay-jay tried to defend himself. Another slap across the face sent him reeling. His head hit the plasterboard with a dull thud and he started to cry. More from the unfairness than anything else.

"I'll give you something to cry about," Ardis muttered, her eyes stupid with alcohol. She came at him again and Jay-jay ducked under her windmilling arms. Ardis bumped into the door sill. She leaned against it, fighting for balance. "Stand still and take what you deserve," she shouted. "Stand still or you're really going to catch it!"

Jay-jay moved warily around the living room, making sure to keep the furniture between himself and Ardis who kept tracking him.

She lunged for his arm across the end table, knocking the lamp to the floor. The bulb didn't break and as the shade rolled crazily, the walls moved back and forth with shadow and light. "Oh, you're going to get it for that," she hissed. "Get over here to me this instant!"

Not on your life, Jay-jay thought. Rebellion began to thud in his chest until it pounded through his entire body. I'll never take anything from you or anybody else ever again!

Ardis feinted for Jay-jay around the television stand and caught his arm. As he tore free from her clawing nails, Ardis' foot caught the tubular leg of the stand. She pitched forward, dragging the set with her.

Jay-jay stood rooted to the spot, watching Ardis and the TV fall as if they were in slow motion. Ardis hit first. Then silver fragments fountained out over the room as the TV screen smashed and the wires and transistors popped out like a jack-in-the-box.

Ardis lay still. The blond wig had fallen off her head and lay on the floor beside her.

Is she—? Jay-jay thought, gone cold with fright.

Ardis started to snore and a sigh of relief escaped from Jay-jay.

He wiped the perspiration from his face, then searched the top of the end table for his eyeglasses. The room came into sharper focus when he got them on.

Jay-jay stared at the wreckage. "If I count to ten and pinch myself . . ." He shut his eyes tight and then opened them. "Glue? Solder?" he whimpered, but knew all the while that all the king's horses . . .

Don't step on a crack from school to home and everything will go okay today. Count to fifty before the traffic light changes and— But all the magic games had suddenly turned into something very different.

"I've got to think of a way out of this! Ardis might wake up any minute!"

Jay-jay groped his way down the linoleum-covered

foyer to the kitchen. He stood on tiptoe and pulled the cord of the overhead light fixture, but the kitchen stayed dark. Ardis must have bulb-snatched the light to use someplace else in the apartment.

Minutes ticked by as Jay-jay stared out the window, trying to dope out a plan. He looked to the black sky and the swirl of stars . . . no help there.

What will she do to me when she wakes up? Jay-jay wondered, and felt his heart contract into a fist.

"I won't take any more from her, I won't!" he exclaimed, and his words fled out the darkened window. Suddenly Jay-jay knew that he couldn't stay in this place another second.

He raced back into the living room, skirting Ardis, who was snoring loudly now. Jay-jay pulled on his old, patched dungarees. Then he hurried through the flat collecting the rest of his meager clothes. Laced up his Captain America sneakers—"Thank God I wasn't wearing them when Elmo got me in the elevator"— grabbed his reversible windbreaker, his pocketknife, dumped his schoolbooks out of his canvas knapsack.

"I won't be needing multiplication tables hitchhiking to California," he said. "I'll meet some other kid and we'll wander all over America together, like on *Route 66*. No, I'll do it alone on a motorcycle like on *Then Came Bronson*. I don't need *anybody!* Nobody will be able to order me to do anything. To brush my teeth. Or take down the garbage. Or not to come home until dark. I'll live on—what will I live on?"

Back into the kitchen Jay-jay ran. Damn! Still dark. He snapped his fingers, opened the refrigerator door and the dim light filtered into the room.

Some brown radishes, wilted lettuce leaves, a jar of mayonnaise turning dark yellow—nothing that made any sense to take. Then he ransacked the kitchen cabinets; crumbs in the Ritz cracker box, and not enough peanut butter left to cover a slice of bread if there'd been one.

"Never mind about that now," Jay-jay breathed. "You've got to get out of here before she comes to. Because if she ever catches you!" Jay-jay was most scared of Ardis *after* a drunk. Because that's when she could move fast. And what was worse, she didn't realize how hard she hit.

"And I'll never come back, never," Jay-jay said, whirling to face all corners of the room.

But deep down, Jay-jay knew that the minute anything went wrong, as soon as he caught a cold, or missed a meal, he'd come running back here with his tail dragging between his legs.

"You know you will, chicken," he muttered. "Because that's the way you are. Did you stick up for your rights when that guy kept fouling you on the basketball court? All Dolores has to do is snap her fingers and you'll go for another Popsicle, right? Remember all the beatings that Ardis dished out? And you'll take more, unless—"

Then Jay-jay did something—if they put him on a torture rack, or bribed him with a ten-speed English racer—even then he'd never be able to explain it.

He tiptoed to where Ardis was lying. With solemn deliberation, he picked up the wig and ripped the rayon strands of hair from the scalp-piece until the floor around Ardis' head was strewn with the irrelevant curls.

Jay-jay zipped up his windbreaker. "I'm never coming

back,'' he said to the wreckage of the room. "No matter what happens. May God strike me dead.''

And then Jay-jay slipped out the door, down the dark winding stairwell and out into the dawning streets to find his life.

Three

Late Saturday afternoon, Jay-jay woke in the park to a gnawing tug on his shoe.

"What!" he cried out, bolting upright.

He saw his attacker then, a scrawny, multicolored pup, who darted away, then dashed in again to attack Jay-jay's sneaker.

Jay-jay shook his leg free. "Dummy," he said. "You can't eat that. Or I would have long ago."

The mongrel didn't believe him and Jay-jay yowled as needle teeth bit through the canvas of his shoe. Jay-jay feinted a kick. "Go on, beat it."

The sun had disappeared behind the buildings lining the west side of the park. Jay-jay shivered with sleep-cold. Groggily he got to his feet and searched for his glasses. When he found them he stuck his fingers through the empty eye frames.

He hunched his shoulders. "Guess I'll just have to learn to get along without them."

Jay-jay's stomach knotted as he stood up straight and he shut his eyes against the dizziness. "Unless I find something to eat, and fast—"

Pins and needles numbed his legs as Jay-jay made his way through the brambles. The dog tracked him warily, ambushing him from a clump of spreading cotoneaster.

Jay-jay picked up a stick and shook it. "Food, clothing and shelter first, and that means I've got no time for you. It's not my fault if somebody left you here to starve. Now bug off!"

Ahead, loomed the mountain of the Great Hill. Up the north incline Jay-jay climbed, holding onto bushes, resting against the nubby bark of a mountain ash. Finally, he made it to the crest. He parted the cover of azalea and sassafrass and peeked. Not a soul in sight.

During the day, the old men and women of the neighborhood would sit here on the plateau of the Great Hill. Some bent Italians would be playing boccie at the long rectangular fields. But at this hour the wide circle of benches were empty.

Jay-jay zeroed in on the trash cans dotting the flat expanse. The first two cans offered no treasure, but in the third, Jay-jay came on a bonanza. The remains of a chicken wing!

"Damn!" Jay-jay shouted and gave chase after the pup who had snatched the chicken from his hand.

"Drop it! You'll choke on the bones!" Jay-jay yelled, but the pup had already disappeared down the slope.

"I'll never let that happen again," Jay-jay swore, once more rummaging through the cans. This time he came up with half a tuna fish sandwich, from the smell of it. And more than a gulp of orange soda left in a can.

Hands trembling, Jay-jay squatted cross-legged on the grass and forced himself to take small bites of the soggy sandwich.

A few more forays into the remaining refuse cans gave him enough food to slake his hunger and thirst. Some crushed potato chips, frankfurter rolls, there were a lot of those, and if he was lucky there was still some mustard on the buns. And the core of an apple.

"Cores are the best part anyway," Jay-jay said to a preening scarlet cardinal perched on a nearby bush. "The seed part, the part that has all the life."

However, Jay-jay made sure he chewed it good. Otherwise, said the Lore of the Streets, you were liable to get appendicitis.

"That's the one thing I can't afford," Jay-jay said, staring at the sinking sun. "To get sick. There just isn't time for anything like that."

For Jay-jay was slowly coming to the biggest decision of his life. Alone, on top of the Great Hill, with the scudding clouds overhead and the day arching toward twilight, Jay-jay felt a moment of such safety that he hugged himself.

The crest of the hill stood taller then the high-rise buildings of Central Park West, and Jay-jay looked far out to the shadowed canyons where he'd spent the day fleeing from Ardis, wandering around and hunting for food. Until he'd gotten so desperate that he'd tried to steal the peach.

"Only this park has been good to me," Jay-jay mused.

With that recognition, the idea that had been forming in his head exploded like fireworks.

"Forget hitchhiking to Florida or California! I'm going to live right here in this park!" Jay-jay exclaimed. "Forever!"

For the space of a heartbeat the world was suspended in that moment when dusk gives way to night. The sun's last light flamed across the sky and then faded to deep blue. The breeze shifted and cooled and September's remaining flowers enfolded. The park lamps twinkled on, small islands of light in the gathering night.

Jay-jay knew that he must be about his business. He jumped to his feet, packed up the food he hadn't eaten and stuffed it into his knapsack.

"Look around, that's the first thing. And before it really gets dark," he said hurriedly. "You've got to find a safe place to sleep tonight." He tried not to admit it, but now that night was almost here he was getting a little scared.

Down the south slope of the hill he slid. Tangled trees and bushes grew like a rain forest and the smell of growth and mulch made his nose twitch.

"Too dark in here," Jay-jay said aloud, trying to keep his courage up. "Couldn't see anything coming. Wouldn't know where to run when the attack came."

The rumor at school was that wild dogs roamed the park at night. They were after the wild chickens that had escaped from the Puerto Rican ghetto families who kept hens for eggs. Maybe, Jay-jay thought. But if not wild dogs, then for sure there were wild people around.

"So don't be too surprised when the attack comes," Jay-jay muttered to himself.

A rustle in the underbrush rooted him in his tracks, and then he bolted without waiting to see what it was.

Better know this area much better before you risk sleeping in there! he told himself.

Down and down Jay-jay ran until he came to the forest's edge. A piece of moon sailed through the sky, and warily he peeked out at a clearing from behind a thick maple tree. The long dark expanse of the Pool stretched before him; the water's edge was fringed with rocks and trees. With the stealth of an Indian scout Jay-jay made his way to the Pool.

"Wherever I decide to camp, it's got to be near a supply of water," he reasoned aloud. "Maybe this spot will do?"

But when Jay-jay finished his thorough investigation he turned thumbs down. Beer cans and garbage floated on the brackish surface. Jay-jay followed the water along its easterly course, making sure to stay behind the protective covering of weeping willow and scarlet firethorn. A wooden bridge spanned the shores and he sped across the sounding planks and came to the Cascade.

The waterfall tumbled down a rocky cliff to whirl and foam its way along the Ravine and then flow through a tunnel. Jay-jay leaped the three steps leading into the cavernous maw. Blocks of cut stone arched around him. He hurried through the sounding tunnel, delighting in the echo that repeated his name. At the other end, the stream ran into the Loch and here the water quieted and looked relatively clean.

"Give or take a Coke bottle or two," Jay-jay said, cupping his hands into the moonlit liquid and tasting it. "Pretty good," he said between swallows. "Like water. Well, if it's poisoned, I'll know soon enough."

Though the water supply was adequate, the place looked too trafficked. Jay-jay left the path and explored a rocky incline. In the dense undergrowth just above the Loch he discovered a small cave. Not much more than an indentation in the earth, but big enough for a small boy.

It was really night now, but Jay-jay forced himself to scout for pine boughs and dry leaves, and with these he lined the floor of the cave. He crawled into the tight space and pulled some more boughs after him until they completely blocked the opening.

"There, finished!" he said, settling back with an uneasy contentment. Only then did he realize that he had to pee. Groaning, Jay-jay reversed the procedure, wormed his way outside and did what he had to do. "I'll never make that mistake again," he muttered.

At last he was settled back in the cave. He put the knapsack by his side and patted it. At least there would be food in the morning.

"Sleep!" he commanded himself.

But his eyes opened wide with every night sound. In the distance a dog's howl bristled the air and Jay-jay felt his skin crawl. How had the Indians managed to survive in the olden days? he wondered. Or Tarzan in the jungle. Or cavemen—

"A fire! If only I could make one," he whispered. "No, that won't work," he told himself. His only hope of living in the park was to keep from being discovered. By the cops, the gangs, the muggers. And Dracula! Jay-jay thought, hearing the sudden beating of wings.

A hundred times during the first hour Jay-jay was on the verge of going back to Ardis. Once he even got to his knees. But the thought of—not the punishment anymore, heck, that smashed TV and the bald wig was worth anything she could dish out—no, it was giving her the satisfaction. And knowing that he had gone back on his solemn oath.

That thought kept Jay-jay in his cave, his head pressed into the bed of leaves. At long last he fell asleep, too exhausted to be terrorized by the dark, by the unknown, and by his loneliness.

Four

A warming touch of sunlight wakened Jay-jay. For a fuddled moment he didn't know where he was. Then he saw the rich brown earth around him, felt the pine needles cushioning his body.

"Snap, crackle, pop," Jay-jay groaned, feeling his bones creak as he stood up. "But—I—feel—great!" he yawned.

He had done it! Spent the night alone in the park and come out alive! Now nothing could convince Jay-jay that the park, the whole soft expanse of it, wasn't giving him special protection.

Out of the cave Jay-jay crawled, into a day golden with dawn. Warblers and thrushes chirped in a stand of basswood and linden; squirrels darted about, searching for nuts in the dew-diamonded grass; the green world was up and busy with the morning's chores.

"What a day to be alive!" Jay-jay said, stretching.

Then Jay-jay spied the mutt that had attacked him the night before. The mongrel was sitting about ten feet away, staring at him with bright dark eyes. And licking his chops. Jay-jay's hand flew to his knapsack.

"The food! You little thief!" Jay-jay yelled and hurled a branch at the pup.

Tail wagging, the dog snatched the wood up in his jaws and brought it back to Jay-jay. But when Jay-jay charged at him the dog got the message and scampered off. Jay-jay went through his knapsack again and searched the cave, on the chance that the mutt might have left some scraps. But the little bandit had gotten it all.

While I was conked out, Jay-jay thought. A whole night's scavenging down the drain. "I can't let that happen again," he said resolutely.

After he'd gotten over his anger, Jay-jay went down to the Loch and did his morning cleanup. Breakfast, thanks to the thief, was a disaster. Just some cracker crumbs and a piece of cheese that had seen better days. Dessert, though, turned out to be something special.

A dozen or so purple finches were eating berries from a choke cherry tree. The tiny red berries were bitter enough to make Jay-jay's mouth pucker. But if the birds are eating them, he thought, shrugging. Afterward his mouth felt tingly and clean.

While he was eating, Jay-jay was disturbed by something that he just couldn't put his finger on. Something unfinished. He ticked off the possibilities on his fingers.

"First of all, you've got to find a new place to live."

Now that Jay-jay saw the cave in daylight he realized that it was much too vulnerable. Magic-marker graffiti was scrawled on a nearby boulder. "Tony Genesis just can't seem to get it together." Graffiti meant people wandering around and that meant discovery.

"So the cave is out," Jay-jay said. "Second and most important thing is to find a reliable source of food."

Maybe I can get my hands on some seeds? Jay-jay thought, scooping up a fistful of earth. Then I could plant—no, a permanent vegetable garden would be a dead giveaway. "Besides, dummy, you can't plant till spring." He let the earth run through his fingers. A nomad, that's what he'd have to be, ranging all over the park in his hunt for food. Until something better came along.

Jay-jay closed his fingers into a fist; the uneasy feeling persisted. "Well," he shrugged, "whatever's bugging me, it'll pop up soon enough. Later, today, tomorrow— Tomorrow! That's it!" Jay-jay exclaimed, feeling a cold shudder sweep his body.

School.

Ardis would never sound the alarm about his running away. What did she care, as long as she got the monthly support check? The social worker wasn't due for her visit for maybe three, four months.

But school. During attendance, they'd call out his name on the Delaney card. Within the week the truant officer would come knocking. Ardis would stall for a few days, but finally she'd have to tell the officer that he'd disappeared. Then the cops would be after him.

"What about you go to class every day?" Jay-jay

asked himself. "Then in the afternoon you come live in the park?"

He weighed that plan for about ten seconds. From what he'd seen the very first day of class, this term would be no different than any of the others. Kids sent to the john in twos to prevent rip-offs by older students. Pot and uppers and downers circulating freely. Frazzled teachers fighting a losing battle to keep order, no matter how many knives and zip guns they confiscated.

School . . . where everybody was bigger than he was. Where everybody was smarter. And even when Jay-jay did know the answer he made believe he didn't so he wouldn't have to hear the teacher say, "Don't wave your hands when you talk. Don't shift from leg to leg. Don't stutter. Don't bang your head with your hands. Don't, don't, don't."

School . . . where he'd gone into a panic every time they had Fractions. And this term there'd be Algebra, with all those unknowns.

Jay-jay shook his head. "Nope. It can't be school *and* the park. It's got to be one or the other. That means I'll have to do something about school. But what?"

The question ate at him all during the day.

The water from the Pool tumbled down the Cascade and coursed into the Loch. Here the currents grew white with turbulence and so Jay-jay was very careful how he constructed his boat.

He folded the sheet of scrap newspaper, watching the headlines disappear into the creases. "Supreme Court Decides. . . ." "Pennant Race Is. . . ."

When he was finished building, Jay-jay christened the

ship *Old Ironsides*, leaned way out over the bank and set her to sail.

"If she reaches the far shore of the Loch without sinking, then I'll be safe," Jay-jay decided, and helped his craft along with mighty puffs of breath.

Jay-jay danced along the shoreline as the boat bobbed and turned in the rushing waters. Halfway there the sail tipped, landed smack in the briny, but then righted itself.

"Make it, you've got to," Jay-jay urged, twisting his body to help guide Old Ironsides through the treacherous rapids.

About thirty feet from the goal the absorbent newsprint became waterlogged. *Old Ironsides* spun around and capsized, slowly sinking to her watery grave. Jay-jay sat down hard on the bank, feeling like he'd just gotten a glimpse of his future.

He punched his palm repeatedly. "School, that's what made the boat sink. I've got to do something about it. Burn the building, like the college guys used to do?"

"No, burning's not my trip," Jay-jay decided as he scuffed his way across the bridle path around 100th Street. "Besides, they'd just get their duplicate records from the Board of Education and then where would I be? Back in the same fix; just can't keep burning down buildings. I've got to figure out a way so that nobody will even suspect that I've dropped out of sight."

Having decided to live forever in the park, Jay-jay spent most of the day reconnoitering the territory. He checked out the sparse comfort stations and the hours they were open; made a mental note of where all the drinking fountains were.

He discovered something important about the food supply. Up in the 100's there wasn't much going on. Squirrels were the clue; they were all scrawny and scared. Poor kids were more likely to torture than feed them. But as Jay-jay worked his way downtown through the park, the squirrels got plumper. And by the time he reached the North Meadow the rascals were sassy enough to come begging for handouts.

Next to school, the other thing bugging Jay-jay was that he couldn't shake that pup! Every time Jay-jay discovered a cache of food, the mutt would either beat him to it or else stand there sad-eyed, growling and wagging that joke of a tail as he watched Jay-jay eat.

Jay-jay considered training the hound to be a hunting dog, or a bird dog, maybe. But all the pup wanted was to free load off him. Or play. "And I've got no time for that," Jay-jay cried, spooking the mutt away.

Baseball diamonds and football fields were cut into the flat plain of the North Meadow. Jay-jay watched the teams in their bright uniforms for a bit, daydreaming of hitting a grand-slam homer, or kicking a ninety-nine-yard field goal.

But they would never be more than day dreams, Jay-jay knew. Something in him would always keep him from being one of those padded kids. The same thing that kept him from being one of the gang at every school he'd attended. He didn't know what that something was, except that it made him sad.

"But I don't have time for any of that, either," Jay-jay said and, shrugging off the mood, moved on.

In a picnic area around Ninety-seventh Street, shaded by a flaming red maple and a Japanese yew, Jay-jay found the remains of a cupcake and half an orange. And sat down to "high tea!" he exclaimed, recalling an old-time English flick on the late movie. "See what the park's doing for me?" he said through a mouthful of chocolate Yankee Doodle and orange slices. "I've never had high tea before."

Another important lesson: Trash cans near picnic areas were more likely to yield a greater variety of food.

Jay-jay came to a gouge in the earth that was the Ninety-seventh Street Transverse. He leaned over the edge of the retaining wall watching the cars whiz by below. He spit at a couple, but only the Lincolns and Cadillacs.

Jay-jay decided not to venture below Ninety-seventh Street. "Not today," he said. "Too crowded with Sunday people."

Besides, he had more important work to do. Jay-jay knew that the home he must find, or build, would have to be in the wildest part of the park. The fewer the people, the less the chance of being found out.

"Better go back and inspect the rain forest surrounding the Great Hill," he told himself.

Despite the urgency, the boy in Jay-jay surfaced and he didn't take the shortest route, but circled around the ball fields toward the East Meadow. Because everything looked cleaner and greener on this rich side of the park, Jay-jay was more conscious of his scruffy clothes. Across the meadow, he saw a kid about his own age running toward him.

The boy was flying the most beautiful kite that Jay-jay had ever seen. An enormous red and yellow butterfly, and some marvel of Japanese invention made it flutter its wings as it soared through the autumn sky.

Jay-jay moved crabwise toward the boy with his long

slick blond hair, brass-buttoned blue blazer and gray flannel trousers. When Jay-jay got to within ten feet of him, the boy stopped running and sent up a message on the nylon string. The small circle of paper spun higher and higher until Jay-jay's eyes blinked with the dazzle of the sun.

Maybe he'll let me hold the string, Jay-jay thought. I'll give it right back to him.

For Jay-jay needed to feel the tug of wings in the air, straining to break free, a freedom that would draw him high up to the heavens.

"Hey," Jay-jay called, "what a beautiful—"

But the polished kid was already running toward the manicured young parents, who were applauding his efforts. Jay-jay watched the mother hug and kiss the kid, watched the father clap him on the shoulder.

"Huh! Look at all that bull the kid's got to put up with," Jay-jay muttered under his breath.

Suddenly, Jay-jay whirled and trained his antiaircraft finger-guns at the sky. Fixing the enemy craft in his sights, Jay-jay sl-ow-ly squeezed the trigger. A burst of ack-ack fire, the streak of tracer bullets found its mark and the alien UFO exploded into smithereens.

Jay-jay shook his fist. "Anything that flies over my territory—" He jammed his hands in his pockets and loped off, oblivious to the speck still lazily sailing in the sky.

The jungle surrounding the Great Hill was less forbidding in the light of afternoon. In fact, Jay-jay thought, weaving his way through the tangle of holly and privet and cockspur thorn, I could live as happy as Yogi

Bear in here. A carpet of painted leaves cushioned his every step and shafts of sunlight lanced through the leafy canopy.

"Well, I tried living close to the earth and that was no good. So what about up?" Jay-jay said, his mind's eye still on the soaring kite.

Jay-jay spent the rest of the afternoon scouting the Great Hill for exactly the *right* tree. A slippery elm looked pretty good, but slippery. When he finally managed to climb up he discovered it was suffering from some kind of blight.

A white birch turned out to be a kick, its reedy branches swayed beneath his weight, swinging him in an exhilarating ride. The evergreens all smelled like Christmas but their prickly spines grew so close together that whenever he turned around in the branches he got stuck. No fun living in an acupuncture tree, he thought.

Unmindful of scraped hands and skinned knees, Jay-jay climbed on, up and down, in and out, discarding each tree in turn; not leafy enough to hide him from the ground; not strong enough to support the house he'd eventually build.

And then he came on it.

"To think that I never believed in love at first sight," Jay-jay murmured as he circled the base of the massive tree. An oak, he thought it was, with a silver shine on its gnarled and nubby bark. The only bad part was that it was a hell of a job climbing it, he thought, as his hands and feet sought purchase in abandoned squirrel holes and protruding knots. But the harder it is, he puffed, the less accessible it is to anybody else.

"Later on, once you've settled in, you'll figure out an

easier way of getting up and down," Jay-jay panted, after he finally managed to gain the lowest limb.

The rest of the climb was a lot easier. There was a kind of resting spot midway in the oak formed by four branches that came together. And that's where Jay-jay decided to stay.

It seemed that this day had just begun and here it was turning dark again. From his vantage point in the tree, Jay-jay watched the blue haze settle across his wild domain. Lark and loon lifted their voices for night's final song and then fell silent.

Jay-jay got comfortable in the crook of the branches, feet stretched out along a thick limb. "No dinner tonight," he said, "but that's okay. I couldn't have eaten anyway, not with the job that's ahead."

All day long the thought of school had gnawed away at him. And now at last he knew what he must do. During the next hours Jay-jay plotted and planned until his course of action was crystallized. Midnight came in on the hollow sounding of distant church bells.

"You've got to do it, there's no other way," he said, trying to psych himself into action.

But he thought of a hundred reasons why he shouldn't leave the safety of the tree. Then, from out of nowhere, something popped into his head that decided him.

When he'd been little and at the orphanage, all the kids had to go to church every Sunday, no matter what their religion. The man preaching the sermon had said something, something that had remained dormant in Jay-jay's mind all these years, waiting for exactly the right moment. Now that moment was here.

Jay-jay climbed down from the oak, scared beyond the

telling of it, but knowing that he must leave the safety of the park, steal through the concrete jungle of the streets, storm the stone fortress of the grammar school, and destroy all his records. Every last one of them. So that not a trace of his old life remained.

It was the only way he could have his new life.

Five

"Nothing to be afraid of," Jay said through clenched teeth, but the ground was alive with shadows and it took him forever to push through the dense underbrush. Over the rise of the hill he went, cutting north across the windswept plateau and then down the north face toward the 106th Street exit.

Rape, robbery, and murder had turned this area into a no-man's-land. Even the gangs thought better of venturing here after dark.

At the 106th Street exit Jay-jay crouched in a clump of Japanese creeper, checking to make sure the coast was clear. Across the avenue, the tall apartment houses were dark. A lone car sped up Central Park West and disappeared with a trail of red light.

Jay-jay sprang from the bushes and sped across the gutter. Keeping in the shadows, he made his way along 106th. In this strange blue-lit stone and steel country he suddenly felt like an intruder.

A black cat, with the secret intent purpose of its kind, crossed the macadam in front of Jay-jay and vanished into a basement.

"Bad luck!" Jay-jay said, and spat three times to break the spell.

As he approached Columbus Avenue a bar blinked a red neon sign on and off. Two people lurched out of the club; a gaudily dressed woman and a man wearing multicolored platform shoes. Jay-jay ducked into a doorway. The couple lingered on the corner, negotiating.

"Can't waste more time," Jay-jay breathed, and taking his courage in his hands crossed the street and hurried by.

At Columbus, Jay-jay turned left and continued downtown until he got to 103d Street. Then right on 103d. Stores were dark and barred, the metal gates and heavy padlocks mute testimony to a land of law and order. The bodega. The pentecostal church. All the landmarks that Jay-jay had passed a hundred times a day now looked weird in the bleached fluorescence of the streetlamps.

"Like the blood's been drained from everything," Jay-jay muttered and ran his tongue around his dry lips.

And then there it was, crouched, ready to spring at him, the three-story structure of his school. Jay-jay skirted the front of the building. Spiked iron fence, padlocked gates. He came to the playground on the west side of the building.

"Playground," Jay-jay snorted. Every recess during

play periods the dealers sold here openly; pot, pills, twenty-five dollars for a bag of heroin the size of a stick of chewing gum.

The play area was separated from the school proper by a chain metal fence. "I'll have to scale it to get to the building," Jay-jay told himself, gauging the height of the barrier at around twenty-five feet. "Fall and you'll break your neck. Come on, now!" he said, kneeling to tighten his shoelaces. "Your records will only be in two places, the Dispensary and the General Office. You can be in and out of there in five minutes."

Jay-jay sucked in his breath and began to climb. Hand over hand, digging his toes into the twanging squares of wire. His hands took on a stipled imprint, his fingers started to go numb, but Jay-jay kept pulling himself up.

At last he straddled the top of the fence. He rested for a second and started down. Easier, but he'd have to find a better way to get out.

"Being hungry can sure knock you for a loop," he said.

The brick walls of the school were scrawled with spray paint. Names: Ronnie, Larry, Teddy. On one totally inaccessible patch of wall an enterprising Michelangelo had managed to write "School Sucks."

Keeping low, Jay-jay scooted around to the rear entrance. Locked tight. All the windows on the ground floor level were locked also. He chose a corner window, braced his elbow like he'd seen on *Police Story* and shoved it against the pane. The brittle crash broke the stillness.

Jay-jay flattened himself against the building, ready to run at the slightest noise. After he'd counted to sixty, Jay-jay reached through the jagged glass and opened the lock. He climbed through the window and dropped to the floor.

It took awhile for his eyes to get used to the dark. "The basement, that's where I am," Jay-jay whispered, recognizing the overhead pipes. With feet as heavy as lead he tiptoed down a long corridor and crept up the stairwell. The same walls, the same tiles, but how different it all felt and smelled. Of Lysol and emptiness. He almost hungered to hear a monitor yelling for quiet.

At the first floor landing, Jay-jay's ears prickled at the sound of a radio. His first impulse was to bolt. Take his chances without destroying his records. Because the music was coming right from the General Office.

Only the memory of the Sunday sermon at the orphanage kept him going. "Come on, now," Jay-jay commanded himself. "There's *got* to be a way! Forget the downhead past. Think!"

Nothing came. His sneakers made no noise as he crept down the hallway. From where Jay-jay crouched he could see through the open door of the General Office. Slouched in a chair, his feet up on the desk, sat Blutkopf, the security guard. Reading a girlie magazine and absently waving his fingers to a lush Mantovani tune. At his elbow was a six pack of beer and the remains of a meatball hero sandwich.

I should have figured that Blutkopf might be on duty, Jay-jay thought.

Though a truce had been declared between the school board and the parents agitating for home rule, the Board of Education didn't trust *anybody* and for the past weeks had posted the cop to prevent a last minute take-over by the militant members of either camp.

None of the kids liked Blutkopf. Pink cheeks and potato nose, he looked like the German commandant on *Hogan's Heroes.* A gleeful laugh rumbled up from his beer gut whenever he manhandled the kids, supposedly frisking them for concealed weapons.

Jay-jay backed down the corridor. A plan still hadn't come to him so he decided to tackle the Dispensary first. He'd seen some records there the opening day of school when the nurse had treated him for impetigo.

Luckily, the health office was in the opposite direction from the guard. Very carefully, Jay-jay turned the doorknob. Locked, also. Snapping open his pocketknife, Jay-jay dug away at the wooden jamb until the bolt was exposed. He pressed the knife blade against the tongue of the lock and the door clicked open.

Jay-jay cocked his head toward the General Office. The radio was still going; no movement. Jay-jay entered the Dispensary, feeling his way around in the dark. The place smelled of medicine. He stifled a yelp as he banged his shin against a metal cabinet.

Too dark to see anything. He'd have to risk a match. He struck one and quickly cupped it in his palm. File cabinets lined one whole wall. He found his class, inched the drawer open and rifled through the folders.

There he was.

Name. Age. Next of kin, that space was blank. Treated for impetigo. The school nurse's comment. "Undernourished. Hostile and withdrawn. Severe antisocial behavior." Recommendation. "Treatment by a child psychologist."

Jay-jay didn't sweat that too much. Not after a five-minute visit. And all the kids had told him she put that recommendation down for every student. Count of she was taking a psychology course at college.

"The heck with you, Hot Lips," Jay-jay muttered. "The heck with psychologists."

He stuffed the manila folder into his pants and cinched his belt tight so it wouldn't fall out. On one of the cabinets Jay-jay spotted a doorstop and pocketed the wedge of rubber without really knowing why.

An impulse sent him back to the files and in the light of another match Jay-jay searched out Dolores' folder. No treatment of any kind, ever. Of course not, he thought, she was perfect. He touched the folder to his lips and then put it back and the cabinet closed with a melancholy click.

Next, Jay-jay went to the medicine cabinet and forced the flimsy lock. "Not that I really want anything in here," he said to himself, stuffing vitamin pills, bandages and iodine into his jacket, along with aspirin, a tube of Vaseline and a shiny pair of scissors. In the morning, when they discovered the door jimmied, Jay-jay wanted it to look as if a pill freak had tried to rip off the place for drugs, but hadn't found any.

Now for the hard part, Jay-jay thought, coming out of the Dispensary. How to get the guard out of the General Office? Sound the fire alarm? Jay-jay looked up to the red box on the wall. His fingers itched to pull the lever, if only for the excitement of it.

Tonight, I, Jay-jay, am starting a new life. And *nobody* is going to get any sleep!

But Jay-jay realized that the fire alarm would be counterproductive. The fire engines would be here in minutes and dozens of people would swarm through the building.

Turn on the hose? It would take Blutkopf a second to turn it off. No, he had to plan a diversion that would lure the guard out of the office, give Jay-jay enough time to lift his records, then get the hell away. And most important of all, without the cop ever seeing him.

But how? How? Jay-jay thought, cracking his knuckles. He jammed his hands into his pockets and his fingers closed around the doorstop. "So that's why I took it!" he exclaimed as the idea sprang into his head.

Elmo had used his foot in the elevator to keep the door *open*. But now—

About thirty feet away from the General Office were the rest rooms. Jay-jay started to slip into the Boys' Room, but at the last second he sneaked into the Girls'. "Why not see something new?" he told himself. Once inside, he looked around with a virgin eye. They didn't have anything you could stand at. Very inefficient, having to sit down every time. "Come on, get on with it," he urged himself.

Jay-jay shut the sink stopper, then stuffed the overflow drain with toilet paper. He turned the faucets on full force, waited until the sink overflowed, and ran out. He sprinted down the hall and ducked into the dark stairwell. Jay-jay looked through the banister rungs and saw a trickle of water seeping under the bathroom door. The stream began to flow toward the General Office.

The radio stopped abruptly. Jay-jay could barely hear anything for the pounding of his heart. Would Blutkopf take the bait? A chair scraped and then the guard called out, "What the hell's going on?" He stepped to the doorway and saw the pool collecting just outside the office.

With the light from the office behind him, Jay-jay saw

Blutkopf's shadow hurtle down the corridor, like some monster with elephant feet and a pin head.

Blutkopf advanced warily, unbuttoning the snap on his holster. "Okay, whoever you are, come out of there with your hands up," he said to the Girls' Room door. But his voice sounded unsure. His hand went to the walkie-talkie hanging on his belt. Should he call headquarters? What would he report? That water was running?

Then Blutkopf snapped his fingers. "A pipe broke, that's all. Or maybe one of the teachers dropped the rag down the bowl. Happens all the time."

Jay-jay pressed himself against the steps. Above the thudding of his heart he heard the slosh of steps, heard the bathroom door swing open, creak shut. An instant of silence.

"Now!" Jay-jay cried, bounding up from the stairwell and racing toward the Girls' Room.

In the lavatory, Blutkopf's eyes took in the overflowing sink. As he reached to turn off the tap he saw the clogged drain and in that moment he realized that he'd been set up. He lurched to get out, but the slippery floor slowed him down.

Just long enough for Jay-jay to jam the wedge under the door even as Blutkopf lunged against it, which only wedged the doorstop tighter.

Blutkopf pounded on the door with his gun butt. He whirled and searched for another way out. No window in the john. Standing ankle deep in the water, Blutkopf swore that whoever had trapped him like this was going to wind up a piece of chop meat.

Into the General Office Jay-jay ran, gobbling the crusts of the hero sandwich as he searched frantically through the files. With the lights on it was a whole lot easier.

"Here it is!" he cried. Thicker this time. Jay-jay

snatched out the folder and stuffed it into his belt along with the medical records. He closed the file drawer, and with an *It Takes a Thief* afterthought carefully wiped away any fingerprints. A box of chalk was lying on the supply cabinet and Jay-jay pocketed it. To make up for the one that Elmo stole from me, Jay-jay thought.

Then he spotted a row of cubicles built against the far wall. In these cubicles were all of the teachers' paraphernalia. God, he'd almost forgotten! His teacher would have his name on a Delaney card!

He searched along the rows until he found her cubicle, slipped out her class book and removed his card. Then he moved the rest of the cards up one space so there was no evidence of his ever having been in the class.

Lucky for him that there'd only been two days of school before the strike started so the instructors didn't know most of their pupils.

"The Health Office, the General Office and teacher's book," Jay-jay said, ticking them off on his fingers. "That takes care of the three places where my name would be."

There was a fourth place, too, the Central Registry of the Board of Education. Not that it mattered, for with the hundreds of thousands of computerized cards and all the inefficient bureaucratic red tape, there wasn't a chance in a million that the disappearance of one small boy would ever be noticed.

Jay-jay jumped at the crackle of the walkie-talkie. Blutkopf must be radioing the police precinct! Jay-jay rushed out of the office and saw that the cop had already forced the bathroom door wide enough to get one hand through. His fingers strained to reach the wedge which lay just out of his grasp.

Jay-jay leaped down the stairwell into the basement. A

small corner of his brain said, "Good, you had enough sense not to get your feet wet." No footprints leading into the General Office and no trail out. Only the Dispensary door was jimmied and that would look like a drug heist.

Through the dingy basement corridors Jay-jay ran, squirming out the back window just as the screaming police cars tore up to the front of the building.

Searchlights were sweeping all over the schoolhouse. Like it's a prison break, Jay-jay thought, peeking from around a corner. If he tried climbing over the schoolyard fence into the playground, he'd get caught for sure.

A searchlight stabbed toward him and Jay-jay ducked. "Give yourself up now," a little voice whimpered as he watched the riot squad pour out of the paddy wagon. But a more compelling voice grated, "Fight it out! Give yourself a chance, something's bound to happen."

Something did. With the arrival of the howling patrol cars, windows up and down the block were flung open. Heads popped out, people began yelling and then the tenements emptied when they saw that the commotion was at their school. In a twinkling, more than fifty people, black, white and Puerto Rican, had crowded into the street. Ladies in their nightgowns, men in undershirts, one heavy-set girl with pink rollers in her coal-black hair.

Curses, complaints and charges flew back and forth. "Wouldn't you know the pigs would break the armistice?" "Try to take over our property?"

From the corner of the school building, Jay-jay watched the swelling crowd grow more hostile. Linking arms, the police formed a line and tried to force·the crowd back while other cops axed the padlock on the front gate.

Jay-jay saw the police line sag and then snap and the angry mob surged through the gate and headed for the front door. Jay-jay took a deep breath. "Here's your chance," he whispered and stepped around the side of the building, quickly mingling with the mob.

Questions and rumors flew around Jay-jay's head. "They caught one of the militants trying to set fire to the school." "They trapped one of the teachers in there, trying to set off a bomb."

Jay-jay squirmed through the mass of people, past the herringboned police cars that blocked traffic. If only Dolores could see me now! In the *Daily News* last week, Confucius had said, "Even the smallest man can cast a giant shadow when the time is right."

"You know it, Confucius!" Jay-jay whispered. He wished he could have stayed around for the television cameras. That girl might even take out her pink rollers. On camera, the cops would become self-conscious and authoritative. "There were reports of this perpetrator and that perpetrator—" Jay-jay could hear them now, like they were reading lines from *Dragnet*.

And then, as though he'd materialized from a nightmare Jay-jay spotted Elmo, the guy who'd mugged him in the elevator.

The commotion had brought Elmo on the run from his rooming house. He'd just come down from a shoot-up high and the street swayed and exploded with each revolution of the police searchlights.

At first, the noise and the crush of bodies frightened Elmo. But he ran his fingers over the loot strung out on his length of rawhide, telling his victories. Completing the ritual, he touched the medallion he now wore around his neck. Elmo took a few deep breaths. He felt good now, he felt an excitement growing in him.

Elmo looked around. This crowd is tailor-made, he thought, a slight smile on his lips. Better check it out. His fingers throbbed with sensitivity. "You might just be able to heist an easy wallet," he said under his breath. True, the cops were all over the place, but that's why nobody would be suspecting anything.

Elmo, his eye on the main chance, wove his way through the milling crowd toward Jay-jay.

"Split from here, *fast!*" Jay-jay warned himself. "Before Elmo or Ardis or anybody else you might know—"

Crosstown and then downtown, Jay-jay made his way back to the park via a new route. In the distance he heard the howlers of more police cars.

"What will happen to that cop?" Jay-jay wondered aloud. Found in the Girls' Room. Especially with the empty beer cans and the girlie magazine. Jay-jay discovered that he felt a little guilty about putting Blutkopf against the wall.

"But on the other hand," Jay-jay reasoned, "Blutkopf isn't a nice guy. He deserves what he gets."

At Central Park West and 100th Street, red pools of light reflected off the black asphalt, then turned green with the changing traffic light. Jay-jay ran across the street and sped through the Boy's Gate. He sprinted around the southern shore of the Pool, jogged over the stone bridge of the Cascade with the yawning blackness of the Ravine below, and didn't stop until he was safe in the forest surrounding the Great Hill.

He found his silver oak and threw his arms around the trunk. "I'll never leave this place again," he swore. "No matter what."

Jay-jay thought of cutting his wrist and sealing his oath with blood. "But you need another person for that, dummy," he told himself.

When he regained his breath, Jay-jay loosened his belt and took out the folders. He laid the records down on the ground in front of him. Despite the danger, he lit a match. Jay-jay watched the edge of the papers curl and brown as the flickering fire stole slowly over the printed matter on the computerized pages.

Name . . . His mother had had two heroes, Pope John and President Kennedy. She felt that it had been a happier, more hopeful time when both men had been alive. Not knowing which of the two to name her son after, she had decided that his first name would be John. And his middle name would be John. In the abruptness of the world, John John had gradually given way to J.J. and finally became Jay-jay.

Father, Caucasian, Deceased . . . He had disappeared into the maw of the war machine in Southeast Asia shortly after Jay-jay had learned how to walk and talk.

Mother, Deceased . . . One of the twenty thousand who died every year, victims of radiation leukemia. Next of Kin, Blank . . . Orphanage. The string of foster homes and foster parents. This charity, that organization.

As the fire ate all of his yesterdays, Jay-jay's body grew tense. It had been a huge victory, and he understood why he'd risked everything.

In the Orphanage every Sunday . . . and all the kids

singing that Jesus loved them . . . and Jay-jay had moved his lips but no sound came out. And so he had sat, mute and defeated by a love that would not reveal itself.

The man in the black robe had thundered, "When you die your soul is freed from your sinful body! Some fall into hell to suffer the fires of eternal damnation. Some of the chosen fly to heaven, there to be reborn. So that's why you have to be good!"

Jay-jay sprang to his feet and stamped at the embers, grinding the ashes into the earth. His eyes swam with tears of anger and hope.

"You don't *have* to die! That's the easy way. There's another way. But you've got to want it, bad. Bad enough to—"

He could not put his feeling into words, but the truth of it coursed through his body, giving him an elation beyond words. Jay-jay scattered the ashes, weaving his fingers through the spiral of smoke that rose toward the stars.

He said slowly, "Jay-jay is dead. Long live Jay-jay."

PART TWO

Six

The start of the new day gave no indication that it would be any different from the days that had passed. Jay-jay had fallen into the rhythm of his new life and within a week it seemed he had never lived anywhere else.

Jay-jay had struck up a definite friendship with his oak. It helped him climb up and down, though that was still a real hassle. The thick canopy of leaves protected him from the sun and enclosed about him at dusk. At bedtime, Jay-jay tied himself to a limb with an old sash he'd found, and every morning he undid the knots. If his bones ached a little for sleeping in the crook of the branches, well, so what? It was better than being bitten by bedbugs.

Food was still the most serious problem. He couldn't

quite get used to always being just a little hungry. Sooner or later he'd have to solve that problem, but he pushed that to the back of his mind, contenting himself for the moment with scraps and leavings.

A problem that he had to solve immediately was that damned pup. Somehow the mutt had sniffed Jay-jay out, and every day he circled the base of the oak, wagging his tail and howling up at the branches.

I really could use somebody to pal around with, Jay-jay thought. But then he curbed this sign of weakness. How would I feed him, when I don't have enough to feed myself?

The dog barked again and Jay-jay tensed. "I just can't let him hang around yowling his head off. He'll attract somebody for sure." Jay-jay climbed down from the oak and got close to the dog. "Poor dumb thing doesn't know whether to bite me or lick my hand. Beat it, go on, now, scram."

The pup wagged his tail furiously.

"This is going to hurt me more than it hurts you," Jay-jay said, sidearming a branch at the mutt. The pup yipped, shot him a betrayed look and scampered off.

"I *had* to," Jay-jay yelled after him. "Otherwise you'd have given away my hiding place."

If Jay-jay had objections to the pup, a squirrel who lived in a nearby elm had definite objections to Jay-jay and voiced his annoyance with shrill pipings at the ungainly creature.

One night the squirrel's curiosity peaked and he raided Jay-jay's oak. Stealing onto the very limb to which Jay-jay had tied himself, the squirrel nosed about, searching for the boy's cache of nuts. But there were none around. Then he went back to his own store that he had gathered for the oncoming winds that would blow from the north, bringing snow and sleet and hunger.

The first light of day filtered through the leaves and the dappled patterns fell across Jay-jay's eyes. He stretched, rubbing his cramped, aching bones. He lay in the branches, luxuriating in the freedom and closed his eyes again. What was the good in running away from home if you couldn't sleep as late as you wanted?

The rustle of leaves murmured, "Wake up," and the shifting patterns of sunlight caressed and warmed his skin. Stomach gurglings finally made Jay-jay sit up. "Pity you're not an apple tree," he yawned, patting a limb.

Jay-jay looked up through the interlocking branches at the sky. Arch upon arch of limbs rose in sweeping arcs toward the blue, and Jay-jay knew a moment of such happiness that he dared not savor it too long, lest something happen to destroy it all.

Early every morning, just after the bells of St. John the Divine began to toll nine o'clock, Jay-jay would see a little bent woman stroll into the park. Down the curving paths she would come, with measured step, for her arthritis always acted up with the approaching cold weather. The lady would take up her position on a bench perhaps a block distant, as the crow flies, from where Jay-jay lived.

For the first week, Jay-jay had considered her an invader into his territory. He didn't mind people *passing* through, but it was another matter if she sat there every morning. It meant he had to be especially careful about being discovered, and he resented that infringement on his freedom.

Some days the old lady would read a book and some days she'd knit tiny sweaters or baby booties and some days she would just bask in the autumn sun. After a bit, sparrows, starlings and pigeons would hop toward her to be fed. And each day the lady would share her crackers with them or crumble the bread too stale for her to eat.

After considerable debate, Jay-jay decided he'd allow her to stay. After all, he reasoned, she wasn't littering or poaching or otherwise making a nuisance of herself. It got so that Jay-jay almost waited for the lady to make her appearance, so comforting a presence had she become.

This day, the old lady came into the park and wandered aimlessly around the paths of the Great Hill, passing close to Jay-jay's oak. From his aerial perch he gazed down at the foreshortened figure; her shoulders seemed more stooped today and her step dragged.

She found her way to her accustomed bench, sat, and took a letter from a vinyl shopping bag. She read the pages slowly and started to cry. Drying her eyes with a frayed lace handkerchief, she heaved a long sigh, then methodically ripped the pages and threw them in a nearby trash can.

The old woman did not pay any attention to the woods creatures who had come to greet her, nor did she stay her accustomed time. Jay-jay realized that her news must be serious.

Don't get involved, he warned himself, but curiosity proved too much. When she had gone, Jay-jay climbed down from the oak and rummaged through the trash can. He found all but two pieces of the ripped letter, the breeze must have carried those away. Jay-jay pieced the jigsaw together, and though some of the words were too long or too hard for him to read, he did manage to get its meaning.

The old lady's name was Mrs. Miller (that's who the envelope was addressed to, so Jay-jay took it to be her name), and she had a daughter living in (return address) Roslyn, Long Island. The letter began.

Dear Momma,

How are you? Well, I hope. Sorry I haven't written sooner but I've been terribly busy. Herman and I have thought it over very carefully and decided that you would be much happier living in the city, rather than the lonely suburbs where you don't know anybody and you can't get around because you don't drive and there's a terrible gas shortage anyway. We thought we might have the extra room since Sonny went away to college but Herman made it into an office, he *had* to, he does a lot of insurance work at home now what with the terrible inflation

A piece of the page was missing here. Then there was a whole paragraph about the children and their whooping cough and chicken pox, and property taxes and expenses, a lot of love and kisses from everybody and the assurance that they'd come visit her very often but not this month because. . . .

Jay-jay scooped up the pieces of the letter and threw them back in the trash can. "Well, I can't start worrying about some old lady too, I got enough on my own," he said, and headed east, where he'd hardly done any exploring.

Past the Glen Span, over the Huddlestone Bridge, and beating his thigh in cadence, Jay-jay slapped leather hard to Fort Fish to escape the pursuing Indians. He climbed the rocky promontory of the Mount—just because it was there!—and stopped to rest in the formal English garden of the Conservatory.

Interns and nurses from Flower Fifth and Mount Sinai hospitals sat eating their lunch amid a riot of flowers. Jay-jay hung around until the starched white people went back to the hospitals, and then he went through the trash cans.

One of the interns had left a red felt marking pen behind and a small yellow pad, and Jay-jay claimed salvage rights. "Finders, keepers," he said through a mouthful of chopped egg on rye and the last of autumn's plums.

It's a pity Mrs. Miller isn't younger, Jay-jay thought, as he wended his way along the boxwood paths. "If only she could be—say around Dolores' age," he said, watching the three green-bronze Graces cavorting in the tiny pool.

Then he could have invited Mrs. Miller to come visit him. But creaking around like she did, she'd never make it up into the tree. Not even if he gave her a boost.

At the rear of the garden, Jay-jay found the Colonial Arcade with medallions of the original thirteen colonies set in the concrete walk. Under the vine-covered arbor, Jay-jay hopscotched from Georgia to Maryland to New York. "We hold these truths to be self-evident," he read from a bronze plaque.

But try as he might, he couldn't push Mrs. Miller from his mind. He wanted to do something for her. But he didn't know what. Visit her where she lived? No, because he'd sworn an oath never to leave the park.

"And you must never break that kind of vow," he warned himself.

Jay-jay flung himself down on the grass and deviled a bunch of black ants trying to cart off the carcass of a grasshopper. Then Jay-jay rolled over and absently looked at his worn clothes.

He beat the dust from his dungarees. Then he snapped his fingers and took off his windbreaker. With the red magic marker he painted a big red sunburst on the back of it. He made the sun come up over the horizon line of the waistband and extended the rays right to the shoulders. When he was done he felt as if he owned a whole new jacket. "Two of them, in fact," he said, "because it's reversible."

An orange polka dot lady bug landed on his hand and when Jay-jay blew at it, it flew off and he knew that it was time for him to go too. The route back took the Sunbeam Kid past Nutter's Battery, around the curve of the Harlem Meer, up a commanding hill where he stared down at the orange accordion roof of the rarely used Lasker Skating Rink. Jay-jay had never been ice skating. Skates were a luxury in his life.

It was still light and it didn't *feel* dangerous, so Jay-jay took the dare and trudged to Lion's Head Rock. Then up the steep mountain to the Blockhouse. Panting for breath, he clambered to the low roofless structure and poked his nose through the slitted windows. A guy and his chick were inside on the hard-packed ground, necking. Jay-jay couldn't decide if he was too embarrassed to watch or too interested not to. An avalanche of pebbles gave way beneath Jay-jay's squirming feet and the guy jumped up, mayhem in his eyes.

Jay-jay fled along the rocky path of the Cliff, holding onto the iron railing sunk into the precipitous stone. Hundreds of feet below, tiny cars sped along the winding West Drive.

"One slip here and you're a goner," Jay-jay breathed. He made it around to the other side of the Blockhouse and then, arms wide, raced down the side of the mountain with the tiniest hope that the wind would carry him aloft to the V's of ducks winging south across the sunset-streaked sky.

Jay-jay stumbled over a log and somersaulted onto his back with a thud. "Oh, well," he groaned, getting to his feet.

His heart beat easier when he got to the familiar territory of the Great Hill. Circling the fringe of the rain forest, he stopped at Mrs. Miller's bench, chewed his lip for a while and then printed in chalk on one of the green slats:

"Dont cry, Mrs. Miller. Its not so bad being by yourself."

"Doesn't mean beans to me if she sees it or not," Jay-jay told himself early the next morning. But it seemed like Mrs. Miller would never show. "Maybe I've overslept?"

Couldn't be, there was the nine o'clock bonging coming from St. John's. Then where could she be? he wondered. Sick? Yeah, that could happen to you a lot if you were feeling blue. In the old days, Jay-jay remembered, he had *always* had a cold. "Maybe she'll never come back?" he blurted suddenly and that thought gave him a twinge. "If only she'd seen my message first."

Just when he'd given up hope, Mrs. Miller appeared. Down the path she came in her slow gait and eased herself onto the bench.

"Without noticing a thing!" Jay-jay swore, slapping the tree trunk.

Jay-jay twisted left and right, trying by sympathetic body magic to make her turn and see. Her elbow brushed the chalk. She started to brush the white dust off her sleeve and—

Mrs. Miller squinted at the bench slat. She shook her head and put on her reading glasses. Still it didn't penetrate. When she finally realized that the message was indeed intended for her, she stared at it with the same reverence Moses might have felt seeing the Ten Commandments.

"What kind of miracle—" Mrs. Miller whispered, her eyes searching the immediate area. Then she saw the pieces of her letter still in the trash can. She stood up then, shading her eyes with her hand and looked at the rolling meadow and the forest behind her.

"Who?" she called, and the faintly rustling trees gave back her call.

Once again Mrs. Miller inspected the message on the bench slat. Judging from the handwriting and the misspellings, it must be somebody very young. And very kind, Mrs. Miller thought, tears welling to her eyes.

Rummaging through her pocketbook, she found the stub of an eyebrow pencil. Underneath Jay-jay's message she wrote in her prim, precise penmanship, "Thank you very much, whoever you are."

Mrs. Miller straightened up and followed the path out

of the park, glancing back at the bench every few feet to reassure herself that she hadn't dreamed the whole thing.

The following morning, when Mrs. Miller hurried back to her bench she was delighted to find chalked under her "thank you," a very brief "your welcome."

She reached into her shopping bag, took out an orange and very carefully placed it on the bench. Then she went away.

Jay-jay waited until she'd disappeared, then scrambled down from the oak and approached the bench. He walked past it nonchalantly, whirled, grabbed the orange in one quick swipe and beat it back to the tree.

It had to be the best orange he'd ever eaten.

Thereafter, whenever she could afford it, Mrs. Miller made a habit of leaving something for her unseen friend. An apple, some cookies, a bologna sandwich. And after ten years of not going near her stove, she even baked a banana bread. If she had known his size, she would have knitted him a sweater. Instead, she started on a long, multicolored scarf.

Seven

Survival was the main event of Jay-jay's days, the never-ending search for food, but some of his nights were filled with adventure.

Where once he'd never been able to get out of bed in time for school, now Jay-jay was wide awake with the dawn. Rarely a day went by when he did the same thing twice, whether it was studying a family of chipmunks, or cheering the sailboat races at the Kerbs Memorial Boat House, or just ranging over the 840 acres of his domain.

On one such exploration, Jay-jay discovered the Bird Sanctuary down at Fifty-ninth and Fifth Avenue. A red-shouldered hawk circled above, a hairy woodpecker rat-a-tatted on a blue beech. Ruddy ducks and green-winged teals paddled on the pond, to upend themselves suddenly and wiggle their tail feathers at him.

For a while Jay-jay played King of the Mountain on a boulder overlooking the sanctuary, fighting off imaginary black knights, but that got boring. He turned his full attention to the birds. It looked like a lot of them were getting ready to migrate.

"How do you know where you're going?" he asked an Iceland gull. He remembered a science show he'd seen on Channel 13, *Nova*. All the bird scientists thought it must be some mysterious homing instinct that human beings didn't know anything about at all.

Jay-jay leaned back on his elbows. "And if I had wings . . . where would I fly to? South?"

Or would he stay here and fight it out the way that chickadee was doing? Jay-jay watched the plucky little bird fight off an iridescent purple grackle intent on stealing its food. The chickadee darted about the intruder, pecking at its head and wings until the bigger bird, wearying of the guerrilla tactics, flew off.

If it hadn't been for the Zoo, Jay-jay might never have returned to the southeast corner of the park. For here the land was tired-looking, trampled by people and cars. Along the paths approaching the animal houses, sat rows of old people, their faces turning with the sun. The same old faces everytime Jay-jay passed there. What were they waiting for? It gave him the creeps. He always felt the need to gallop back to the wilderness of the northwest park where a kid could still breathe.

But Jay-jay couldn't get along without a regular visit to his animal friends. He wiggled his ears at the lumbering elephants, pinched his nose at the smelly camels. Feeding time for the seals was always a spectacular. At first, Jay-jay applauded with the rest of the crowd when the tear-drop animals honked and clowned for their meal. But as the days passed, Jay-jay got angry at them. For performing.

"Yes, sir, no sir, I'm sorry, sir, I'll never do it again, sir," Jay-jay muttered under his breath, remembering a couple of the places he'd been. "I'll never knuckle under like *that* again," he said resolutely, "not even to eat."

Jay-jay spent hypnotic afternoons at the cage of the black leopard, watching it pace back and forth. He learned a lot about leopards, that its tail was as long as its body, that it perspired through its tongue, and that when some dumb cluck pestered it, its topaz eyes turned blood red.

"Carnivore," the sign on its cage read.

When Jay-jay asked a zookeeper what that meant, the man said the leopard ate meat. Staring at the yawning mouth and the jagged teeth, Jay-jay didn't find that hard to believe.

Jay-jay's eyes met the cat's. "If I could let you out," he whispered. "You and the rest of the animals. . . ." Out of their cells, like he was.

Often, Jay-jay wandered around the menagerie until the shadows of the trees slanted east with day's end. Bronze fairy-tale characters that he now knew by heart danced around the chiming Delacorte Memorial Clock, tolling the twilight hours.

A few diners sat beneath the gay red and white awning of the Cafeteria. Jay-jay waited until no waiters were in sight, then ran down the rows of outdoor tables, snapping up the remains of french fries and bits of hamburger. His cheeks were bulging and his pockets full before the waiters charged out of the dining room and chased him away.

"Got to be a better way of getting food than this,"
Jay-jay said, burping all the way back to the Great Hill.
"Think!"

On a dank, chilly day in October, Jay-jay made a
discovery that changed his entire life. He was heading
down the bridle path along the west side. Just above the
treetops at Eighty-second Street, he could see the
block-long buildings of the Museum of Natural History,
and the dome of the Planetarium.

Though he had to cross the avenue to get to it, Jay-jay
rightly considered this area to be part of his Central Park
domain. A general astride a horse guarded the entrance
and Jay-jay saluted him smartly as he went into the
museum.

What an eye-opener the place was! Jay-jay spent the
day there, wandering through the rooms jammed with
exhibits. Imagine, a whale that filled a whole auditorium!
He felt the hairs on the back of his neck bristle as his
eyes traveled up the fifty-foot skeleton of *Tyrannosaurus rex*, "The largest carnivore ever to roam the
earth," the plaque said.

Jay-jay stared at the monster's open jaws. They were
a hundred times bigger than the leopard's. And the rows
of teeth? Each a foot long, at *least*. "Now *that's* a
carnivore," Jay-jay gulped.

Why had God made some animals eat only grass, like
Brontosaurus, Jay-jay wondered, while others, like
Tyrannosaurus ate meat? And how come human beings
ate both? Did that make man twice as good as everybody
else? Or half as good? It was something to really puzzle
over.

It was at the exhibits of early man that Jay-jay made

his most important discoveries. He pressed his nose against the glass window of the cyclorama.

Ingenious, the way the Zunis had built their cliff dwellings, connected to the ground by a series of ladders. At the first sign of trouble, all they did was haul up the ladders and the enemy had no way of reaching them.

"That's almost like me living up in the oak," Jay-jay said, his breath fogging the glass. Of course, he couldn't use ladders, they were too cumbersome and visible. But sooner or later he'd dope out an easier way to get into his tree.

In the next exhibit, nomadic tribes used hides from buffalo to construct tepees. Still others built their homes on stilts over lakes. The ideas churned in Jay-jay's head until gradually a hazy picture of what he must do began to form in his head.

By the time he got around to it, it was too late to catch the last show at the Planetarium. But Jay-jay promised himself that one day soon he'd find out what went on in there.

On a clear night of the full moon, Jay-jay journeyed downtown to the Wollman Memorial Rink. Under the umbrella of light he watched the skaters, girls with short skirts that flared as they turned, guys with bright sweaters. For a brief moment the skaters were transported back to the time of the waltz.

Jay-jay waited until everybody was gone, even the watchman, and all the lights were off. Then he climbed the fence and gingerly walked to the center of the rink. The pale moon pulsed down, turning the ice phosphorescent. Jay-jay took off his sneakers and did a tentative glide in his stockinged feet. Gaining courage, he clasped his hands behind his back the way he'd seen the Olympic skaters do; faster and faster Jay-jay sped, outdistancing his pursuers, winning every race.

Speed gave way to art and Jay-jay imagined Dolores in his arms, and they were waltzing. "It would be better with music," he said, and tried to hum "Tenderleaf Tea." But Jay-jay still couldn't sing. When he fell a couple of times, Jay-jay decided that Dolores was a klutz.

He twirled about until his socks were soaked clear through. He looked down at his frozen toes and for a moment panicked with the thought that he might catch cold.

"Never," he told himself, cheeks flushed with exertion. "I'm too happy to catch cold."

October, passing through, withered leaves.

One morning Jay-jay woke up feeling mean. He didn't know why he felt so mean and lonely, he just did. And why this day more than any other? He didn't know that either.

He untied the rope around his waist and stretched. All his muscles felt sore. "I can't take much more of being tied to this trunk," he muttered. Along with his constant fear of falling, the temperature had dropped during the night and that added to his discomfort.

Jay-jay rubbed the blood back into his hands and feet, then climbed high into the leafy bower. From the vantage point he surveyed the countryside. Still too early for anybody to be about. Jay-jay looked to the sky to decipher the day. Pale yellow in the east where the sun was rising, giving way to a serene blue overhead.

He leaned back against the tree trunk. His nostrils contracted to the sharp air, heady with the fragrance of leaves turning, of days descending toward a time of year that had always made him feel sad.

From some distant reaches of childhood, Jay-jay remembered a fairy tale about a hungry princess who had snitched six pomegranate seeds and that was why the leaves fell and for six months everything died.

"And what will happen when the leaves fall from my tree?" Jay-jay thought suddenly. Then he would be visible to the prying eyes of the world.

Jay-jay hit the branch with slow determined slaps. "I will *not* be lonely," he insisted, and immediately sank deeper into his mood.

Though he didn't realize it, weeks of always being a little hungry had taken their toll. The whole world seemed out of sync, and the rustle of leaves today seemed not at all friendly, but harsh and discordant.

"Look at Jay-jay," they whispered. "Lazy Jay-jay."

"Oh, yeah?" Jay-jay yelled back. "Well, I feel mean today too, so watch out!"

For a short time he hung in the branches. Then, balancing himself against the trunk, Jay-jay unzipped his fly and peed, watching the golden stream arch from his arched body and fall to the ground far, far below. But the thrill he usually felt when he did that did not come over him this time.

"If only I had a brother," Jay-jay said, zipping up. "Somebody to hang around with. Even a sister might do," he admitted grudgingly. "If only I had a father," he called to the leaves. "Then you'd see. Yeah. Or a mother. Even a friend. If only I could fly away from it all!"

"If only! If only!" the leaves crackled back in their many voices and the branches added their deeper complaint about the boy who was too lazy to feel anything but sorry for himself.

Jay-jay tried to interest himself in a chickadee flying back and forth, busy, busy, collecting grasses and twigs and seeds for the dark months ahead. But the constant blur of wings only made his eyes hurt.

In the adjoining elm, neighbor squirrel scurried into view, up and down the trunk of his tree he went, cheeks bulging with a supply of nuts. The squirrel stopped to fix Jay-jay with a beady eye. And its flashing eyes that reflected the morning seemed to say, "Look at this bright and blue and golden day! Only a fool could feel mean and lonely!"

Jay-jay picked up a piece of bark and threw it at the animal. The squirrel sat up straight on its hind legs, paws cupped down in front of his white bib. His nose twitched disapprovingly. Then he went on about his labors with a disdainful toss of his tail that implied, "I have no time for the foolish games of silly boys. Who *want* to be lonely."

Jay-jay shook his fist and yelled after him, "If ever I catch you—" He watched the roller coaster tail disappear.

Jay-jay made a sound midway between a sigh and a groan. He didn't even care if Mrs. Miller showed up today. "Not even a friend," he said to himself. "Only me."

And then for some unexplainable reason Jay-jay got very angry. "Only me," he repeated. "Me!"

For a dizzying moment the short span of his years telescoped, blurred recollections of faceless people, some kind, some cold, some nothing. How his hope had jumped with each one. Maybe he would be lucky this time? How his hope had died. Each time throwing him back on himself.

"Me," Jay-jay repeated, and then with a sudden resolve that lifted his spirits he exclaimed, "Yes, that's right! Me. *I* am going to be my own good luck! That's right, *me!*"

Head working feverishly, Jay-jay climbed down from his lookout post to the spot where he'd spent the night, where the thick branches grew out from the trunk forming a sort of platform.

He would make this his kingdom. To make this his kingdom he must build a castle. The gurgling brook below and the waterfall would be his moat. The outcropping of boulders and rocks were the perfect battlements. From the towering point in the highest tree on the Great Hill he would be able to see the approach of any enemy. All that was lacking was the castle. And that he would build.

A castle close to the sky. Whose walls would be of living leaves. Whose supports would be of sturdy oak, alive and growing around him. Growing with him. And when he was done building his castle in his kingdom—

Birds stopped their chatter, butterflies lit all about, squirrels bounded over, all drawn by the strange new electricity coming from Jay-jay's tree.

And as the hope surged in Jay-jay, the branches bowed and nodded and the leaves sang him on, "Yes, Jay-jay, yes."

"When I am done," Jay-jay said, hitting his chest, "then I will decide who I will let in. Yes, me."

Never again would he be the beggar at the door. Never

again would he wait for the kind word. For the pat on the head. For the simple touch to let him know he was wanted.

From this very moment he would become all powerful. From this very moment, tall and princely. From this very moment he was Jay-jay, the Prince of Central Park.

The leaves turned, and withered. But they did not fall. For some reason known only to the tree, they remained on the branches turning from their greens to golds to russets. But they did not fall. And long after the other trees in the park were stripped bare, naked to the penetrating winds, the leaves on the guardian oak stayed, sheltering him from the prying eyes of the world.

Eight

Mrs. Miller picked her way down the pitted stone steps of her rooming house. She nodded to the slight, olive-skinned janitor who had just put out the garbage.

I must learn how to say good morning in Puerto Rican, she thought. Through the years she had learned to say it in German, Italian, Yiddish. So why not Spanish? The janitor disappeared into the basement.

"In the old days they used to sweep the sidewalks," Mrs. Miller clucked. But then they used to do a great many things in the old days. Nor did it do any good to complain, she knew. Because then everybody ran away from you.

A gust of wind whipped her coat and she knotted her scarf tighter around her head. There was an edge to the air today. With the confusion of daylight saving time, Mrs. Miller always felt as though she had misplaced an hour. She thought of her friend in the park and she shuddered with the chill.

"What does he do when it rains?" she asked, making a clucking noise. "What will he do when it snows?"

Mrs. Miller was almost certain that it was a he. The daily handwritten messages he left had a bold stroke, but also the hesitation of a youngster. A child almost, she guessed.

"It's a thing to marvel about," Mrs. Miller said. In the weeks they'd been corresponding, she'd never seen him. Yet, whenever she went to her bench, she felt his presence.

As she hurried along to do her morning errands, Mrs. Miller pondered the questions she had written on the slats of the bench.

"Won't you let me see you?"

"No," he had answered.

"Why not?"

"Because."

"How old are you?"

"*Very* old."

"Where do you go to school?"

"The park is my school."

"Where do you live?"

He had not answered her question that day, and Mrs. Miller was frightened that she had scared him off. Or worse, that something had happened to him.

She had asked her next question with trepidation.

"Where are your parents?"

He had answered: "I don't have any."

"Who takes care of you?"

"Me "

"What do you eat?"

"Whatever I can."

"Please, won't you tell me where you live?"

"In a place where I can see you but you can't see me."

Mrs. Miller waited for the light to change, then crossed Amsterdam Avenue. Though it was a mystery beyond her comprehension, she now felt certain that her unseen friend lived in the park. Yesterday she had asked him a most important question and she was very anxious to see if he had answered it.

A cigarette butt sailed out of a third-story window and narrowly missed Mrs. Miller. "You should be ashamed of yourself!" she yelled up. She shook her head sadly at the rows of scabrous buildings. When she and Max had first moved here they had been lovely one-family houses. Or floor-through apartments like her own.

With the years they had become the domain of the slum landlords, the spacious high-ceilinged rooms divided into tiny cubicles so that the people who lived on fixed income, or welfare, could be packed tighter into the rental spaces.

"But it must be dangerous for a little boy to live like that!" Mrs. Miller blurted. Ah, if Max was alive he would have found a way to locate her elusive stranger. Who but Max would listen to her suspicions about a baby living in the park? "Ah, Max, Max," she sighed. If he was alive . . . then she wouldn't be getting such letters from her children on Long Island.

"Not that I would ever live *with* them, never!" she said to her reflection in the drugstore window. Her own apartment, what else? But they were frightened even of that. She didn't blame them, really, for they had their lives to live out and she had her long journey to prepare for. Most of all, she missed the little children. Something about them, the way they were walking, talking, reading, growing, made her days sunnier.

The long years of Max's illness had cut deeply into their savings. After the funeral, Mrs. Miller had given away most of their furniture to the Salvation Army, and moved into a two-room kitchenette. Less to clean, she told herself. But the four walls had become more and more oppressive and so the park was more vital to her than ever before.

"How could it be that he lives in the park all the time?" Mrs. Miller mused as she passed the grammar school. It was recess and swarms of children were playing ball and yelling. "How could he get away with it, not going to school?" she asked, shrugging. "They're just not making truant officers like they used to."

Such a commotion they had had here last month, with the police and mobs and—unh! What had happened to the simpler days when a school had been as much a sanctuary as a church? Everybody was going crazy, that was what.

Mrs. Miller tightened her grip on her pocketbook and hurried toward the bank. The first days of every month were the most dangerous times in the neighborhood. That was when the Social Security checks arrived, and that was when the crooks and addicts prowled the streets. Waiting for the old people to come from the supermarkets with their groceries. Waiting for the old people to come from the bank with their cashed checks.

"Now stop thinking such nonsense," Mrs. Miller said. "There's nothing to be afraid." She glanced around. There didn't seem to be anybody suspicious in sight.

Reassured, she reminded herself of the TV editorial she had heard on the *Six O'Clock News.*

The newsman had said that if more people walked the streets there would be less crime. That, in effect, there was nothing to fear but fear itself. She had believed it when Roosevelt had said it. But nowadays it seemed like everybody was a crook, from the meanest thief to the highest politician.

But what can I do about that? Mrs. Miller had asked herself. Whatever you can, she'd answered. So this month, instead of mailing her check to the bank, she decided to cash it herself. It would save her ten cents for a stamp, they should drop dead for raising the rates, and another fifteen cents by not having to cash a personal check at the supermarket. Twenty-five cents in all.

"And I'll buy him something nice," she decided. "Something really nice."

Mrs. Miller hated scrimping like this. She and Max had planned for their retirement, and she would have felt easier except for the terrible prices on everything.

Mrs. Miller arrived at the bank just as the clock struck nine. A guard unlocked the door and she went inside. She waited patiently while the tellers unlocked drawers and cabinets, turned on lights and otherwise prepared for the day. She did not notice a thin young man at one of the writing desks going through the motions of filling out a deposit form.

As the predator comes to the water hole at times of drought, so Elmo came to the bank on Social Security day. His eyes darted about furtively, checking out the customers, trying to get the feel of who would be the easiest mark.

A month ago, Elmo had celebrated his seventeenth birthday. He might have been a beautiful youth; there were still traces of it in the fine bony structure of his face and in the guarded vulnerable look in his enormous yellow eyes. But two and a half years of riding the white horse had burned out his brain.

The constant sniffling had made his eyes red and watery and angry lesions blotched his skin. But Elmo never thought about his appearance anymore, the way he no longer thought of being a landscape gardener or a forest ranger. His high school adviser had looked at him like he was crazy when Elmo talked about that. To say nothing of his buddies. For there were only three ways out of the ghetto: show business, sports, or drugs. And since he had no talent in the first two, Elmo had drifted into the third.

It did make his life simple, splitting it into periods of blackness and light. Black, when he didn't have enough bread to score, when he took tremendous risks robbing people at knife point. Light, when he managed to buy a bag and felt the first rush of warm blood creep through his body and color his brain into something warm and sensuous. It was better than getting laid, it lasted longer. And he had dreams of such glory that emperors might have considered themselves rich to dream them.

But each time it took more and more heroin to send Elmo up, and each time a little more of his reason melted away. The new laws had made dope harder to find on the streets, and what with inflation, he needed about forty dollars a day to support his habit. Generally, Elmo operated in Brooklyn and the Bronx. Purse snatching, occasionally mugging a drunk; subways late at night were sure to turn up an easy mark. But for some reason

Elmo hadn't made a hit in two days and he knew he only had a few hours more before he went into withdrawal.

Desperate, he'd come back to his own neighborhood, knowing it was the first of the month. Elmo's eyes skipped over a short white-haired lady on the line and fastened on a young secretary. The teller finished loading a leather pouch with stacks of bills and handed it to the girl.

Must be a couple of hundred dollars in there at least, Elmo thought. Maybe even a thousand. Payroll, probably, for one of the small businesses that still clung on in the neighborhood. A garage, or an auto showroom.

Elmo watched the girl move out of the bank. He forced himself to wait a couple of beats and started after her. Imagine not having to go out on a job for two, three weeks? Not having to fence his loot with his pusher for a tenth of its worth? Imagine just hanging loose and not having to hassle anybody, hurt anybody?

The jewelry on the leather thong jingled and clinked as Elmo jammed his hands into his pockets. His fingers catalogued the loot prayerfully. Let it go easy this time, please, Elmo thought. Let there be a lot of money in her pouch.

Elmo zipped out of the bank's revolving door. Damnation! The girl was heading toward a double-parked car; a bodyguard-type dude slouched at the wheel. For a second, Elmo calculated the percentages. Dark, and he would have snatched her pouch in an instant. But with daylight, the bank guard just inside and the big mother in the car—

A slow stain of panic began to spread through Elmo's body. He *had* to score. Already the pains in his gut told him he had an hour, two at the most. Beads of sweat broke out on his forehead as he watched the car roll away.

"Excuse me," the tiny white-haired lady said, moving around Elmo, who was blocking the revolving door.

His eyes went to the pocketbook looped over her arm. She started down the street. Elmo began to stalk her.

Elmo followed Mrs. Miller for two long blocks, staying maybe fifteen yards behind her. Poised for the exact moment when he would bolt forward and grab her purse, for he had refined his work to an art. But every time he made his move, somebody came from the other direction, or she crossed the street, or like now, she'd stopped at the street-front counter of a candy store.

Elmo hiked his foot onto a johnny pump and made believe he was tying his shoelace, all the time watching her from the corner of his eye. "Now what in the world would an old lady want with such a big chocolate bar?" he muttered. "And a giant balloon?"

Mrs. Miller was feeling very positive about her decision to go to the bank. She'd deposited all but ten dollars in her account. Then she'd gone into the telephone booth in the bank, had put the crisp single dollar bills into a small chamois purse and pinned that to the strap of her brassiere.

Later in the day, when all the deliveries had come in to the supermarket, she'd go and buy her food for the week. She hoped they still had the sale on chicken. So, she would have accomplished what the television program said she must do.

"They're right," she said, shrugging. "There's really nothing to be afraid of. A lot of it is in people's minds."

And when you get older, Mrs. Miller thought ruefully, then it seems to be in your mind a lot.

As she turned onto Central Park West the wind nearly ripped the balloon from her hand. She smiled as she watched it bob in the air. "What a mad, foolish thing to buy!" she exclaimed, tugging on the string. "I hope he likes red," Mrs. Miller said as she hurried through a cyclone of leaves at the 106th Street entrance of the park.

Elmo waited until the old lady was inside the park before he followed her across the avenue. He couldn't believe this piece of luck! Imagine her chancing the park at this empty hour? There weren't even any dog walkers in sight. God must have sent this old lady across his path.

Nine

Along the path, down the winding steps, down through the years Mrs. Miller went. Imperceptibly, her body seemed to straighten, her midsection slimmed to an hour-glass figure.

"Am I getting mixed up in the head?" she wondered, as memories crowded into her head. But spring proved more potent than winter and she heard the brasses of concerts, saw girls in long dresses floating along the Mall, remembered when the most important item in a girl's wardrobe might be her hat.

How Max had courted her during those innocent days. Together they had blown at the feathery heads of dandelions, wishing on the pods that flew off into the future.

The weekdays led to Sunday for the Sunday park was

their oasis. Over to the Sheep Meadow they'd wander to watch the curly lambs grazing. Or they would go dancing at the Pavilion. Two left feet Max had, but he suffered the Castle Walk and the Peabody because she loved it.

But then the Pavilion burned down. When? Mrs. Miller wondered. Was it twenty years ago? Forty? She heard the clip-clop of horses on the turf, saw the gentle halo of lamps as they shone their muted light on strolling lovers. A week before she and Max were married, she had let him touch her for the first time in the park. And she had never regretted it.

Then there had been that grim time when thousands of Hoovervilles had mushroomed all over the park. The authorities complained bitterly about the desecration, but they'd let the squatters live there anyway because the alternative was revolution.

One by one the sheep had disappeared. People do terrible things when they're hungry, Mrs. Miller thought.

When the children started coming, Mrs. Miller had wheeled their baby carriages along these paths. They were hard-packed clay then, not this bleak gray asphalt, and there were no high rises squeezing in from all sides. Once inside the park all you saw was grass and trees and sky and you could forget there was a city beyond the green. And hardly any automobiles careening around and no litter and no—

The balloon bounced and jerked at Mrs. Miller's finger. Mrs. Miller shrugged. "I'm complaining again. But after all, what's left of the park is better than nothing."

Lost in reminiscences, Mrs. Miller did not notice that Elmo had closed the gap between them. She came to her favorite bench and tied the balloon string to a slat.

She scanned the bench eagerly to see if her friend had

responded to her question: "Won't you tell me your name?"

And there was his answer!

"The Prince of Central Park!" Mrs. Miller murmured, overcome with awe.

Only when Mrs. Miller turned to sit did she see Elmo approaching. Almost at once she knew. Her hand flew instinctively to her bosom.

In one fluid motion Elmo struck, ripping the pocketbook from her hand. An unspoken message flowed between their eyes. If she resisted he would kill her.

Mrs. Miller knew it would do no good to scream. There wasn't a soul in sight. Elmo snapped open her purse, rummaged through the compartments. Nothing! Except some loose change. Her Senior Citizenship Card for half fare. Who to Notify in Case of Accident. A couple of photos of kids.

Elmo thrust his head at her. "Where is it? I saw you in the bank. They gave you money. Where is it? I don't want to hurt you," he said, louder this time, his voice quivering somewhere between a threat and a plea.

She would have told him if she could, but fright kept her throat paralyzed. Her fingers crushed the chocolate bar into a shapeless mess. She looked down at her hand and a terrible thought crossed her mind.

Could this be her unknown prince? Had he lulled her into a false sense of security all these weeks only to trap her like this?

Her hand trembled as she held out the chocolate bar toward him. Elmo slapped it away. His eyes swept over her like a scanner. Not wearing any jewelry. Bad. It meant he'd have to go to another part of the neighborhood in order to score. Because if he let her go she'd blab to the cops for sure and they'd be on the lookout. The thought of all the time he'd wasted tracking her sent the pains shooting faster through his body.

"Where is it?" he shouted, losing all control. He grabbed her shoulders and shook her. Mrs. Miller screamed then and Elmo hit her. She fell to the ground and struck her head.

Did I kill her? flashed through Elmo's mind as he knelt beside her. Thank God she was still breathing. "Sometimes they hide the money," he grunted. "In their shoes or in their underwear." He hiked up her skirt. Nothing in the top of her stockings.

He fumbled with her brassiere. His fingers tore at the loose old flesh—there it was! Pinned to her brassiere strap.

From his sentinel lookout high in the oak, Jay-jay had seen Mrs. Miller wending her way along the paths. His heart leaped at the sight of a great red balloon towing her along. Bright as the sun it was in the cold mizzle of this October day.

A stand of willow saplings hid her from view for a bit and Jay-jay waited impatiently until she was pulled into view again by the balloon. Why would an old lady be playing with a balloon? Jay-jay didn't dare hope that she— He jerked alert at the sight of a guy following the old lady, coming up fast from behind.

The hackles on Jay-jay's neck rose. The guy was going to mug Mrs. Miller, that was for sure. Conflicting feelings clashed in Jay-jay. He wanted to warn her and at the same time damned the day he'd been curious enough to read her letter and to have gotten involved. A month of fruit and cookies and sandwiches urged him to save her.

Yet if he yelled he'd give himself away. All that he'd so carefully worked for these past weeks would be destroyed. Once anybody knew where he lived he was a goner.

"Wait a second!" Jay-jay exclaimed. Something about this guy was familiar. From this distance Jay-jay couldn't quite make out his face . . . but the way he kept hunching his shoulders—In Jay-jay's mind, he saw the nylon stocking stretched over the guy's head, turning the features into an unrecognizable blob. Elmo. The lowlife who'd ripped him off in the elevator.

That made it doubly dangerous. If he showed himself Elmo might recognize him. See where he lived. And Jay-jay certainly couldn't afford to let *Elmo* know he was living in the park!

As he battled with his conscience, Jay-jay watched Elmo close the gap. Jay-jay tried to look away. It's none of your business what have old people ever done for you don't get involved!

Mesmerized, Jay-jay stared at them. It was like watching a leopard ambush an old deer. There was never any doubt how it would end. Jay-jay saw Elmo spring. Saw Mrs. Miller's body stiffen. For a second it looked as if they were playing statues. The old lady with her fist pressed to her chest, Elmo, his hand outstretched, demanding. Floating above them, the balloon bounced around in its irrelevant wind patterns.

Elmo broke his rigid stance, his mouth worked and his fist swung through the air. Mrs. Miller screamed as she fell, an old, tired scream. Jay-jay was positive that somebody had heard her. Heard her scream and would come running. But nobody came running.

"Not even you," Jay-jay whispered.

Elmo was bending over the old lady, fumbling with her dress. Whatever fears Jay-jay had for his own safety, whatever his reservations about being discovered, all of these vanished when Elmo touched Mrs. Miller.

Jay-jay scrambled down the tree, swearing at himself for having waited so long. By the time he got to them it might be too late. Jay-jay leaped the final few feet, running before his sneakers touched the ground. Halfway down the hill he scooped up a thick fallen branch without breaking his stride.

Some inner mechanism warned Elmo that everything wasn't A-okay. Too light out, too open for what he'd done. But he didn't have any other choice.

Once more he searched the rolling meadow, glanced over his shoulder at the trees covering the steep hillside. Nobody in sight. Trembling with anticipation, he opened the old lady's chamois bag.

"Maybe she's got some jewelry in it?" he breathed hoarsely. That would be neat. Maybe enough to keep him off the streets for three, four days.

Elmo dumped the contents on the ground and then sat back hard on his haunches. Only ten single-dollar bills! A thin worn wedding band, worth maybe a buck at the most. Not another thing!

By the time Elmo realized that somebody was running up behind him it was too late. Elmo turned in time to see a kid—a little kid! Caught a fleeting glimpse of his face just before the branch clubbed him over the head. Elmo pitched forward, stunned. Half-conscious, but unable to move, his swimming eyes focused on his attacker. Unbelievable! A little kid! Then Jay-jay turned and Elmo saw a great big splash of red on the back of his windbreaker.

Jay-jay wrestled the money from Elmo's clenched fingers. All of a sudden Jay-jay stopped. He spotted a medallion around Elmo's neck. His medal!

He grabbed the chain and yanked it over Elmo's head. He wanted to kick him, to punch him. To yell, "See? I got it back and you'll never get it away from me again!"

But Jay-jay could do none of these things, for Elmo's dazed eyes were following his every move. And Jay-jay was scared to death of those pale yellow eyes.

Jay-jay turned to Mrs. Miller. He pulled her bodice up to hide her brassiere and her skirt down to hide her panties. Pulling and tugging, Jay-jay tried to drag her out from Elmo's dead weight.

Mrs. Miller surfaced from her dark fall feeling tiny slaps on her cheek. She opened her eyes—a little boy—she thought it must be a little boy, he was too dirty to be anything else.

She blinked her eyes and in that instant he was gone. So was the chocolate bar she'd had clutched in her hand.

Mrs. Miller felt a heavy weight pinning her leg and raised herself to see her attacker sprawled across her. The crumpled dollar bills lay in her lap along with the chamois bag and her wedding ring.

Whimpering, Mrs. Miller crawled out from under the young man. She retrieved her pocketbook and stuffed her money into it. A terrible pain throbbed in her head and her whole body felt stiff and sore. She knew she was going to be sick but she weaved along as fast as her wobbly legs would carry her, giving feeble yells every few steps.

A police car cruising along Central Park West saw her stumble from the park and collapse against the concrete retaining wall.

Mrs. Miller managed to tell the policemen what had

happened. She pointed deep into the park. "The bench with the balloon," she blurted and then fainted.

One of the cops radioed for an ambulance, the other ran into the park, gun drawn. But when the policeman reached the bench with its gaily bobbing balloon there wasn't anybody there.

A quick search of a nearby clump of winterberry bushes netted Elmo. He sat slumped over, rubbing a big knot on his head. Before he could resist Elmo was handcuffed and hustled out of the park, fighting and yelling about his rights every step of the way.

Booked at the precinct house, Elmo vehemently denied the old lady's charges. "I don't have any money on me, do I? It's just some crazy lady's story against mine, right? And she isn't even here!"

As for the tracks on his arm, well, sure he'd been strung out. But he was just about to join a methadone program when the cops busted him. "For doing nothing more than sitting in some bushes minding my own business!"

After the police surgeon gave Elmo a shot of methadone to keep him from collapsing, Elmo was taken down to the Tombs. He had never been jailed before and the confinement almost freaked him out.

At the emergency ward of Flower Fifth, the nearest hospital to the crime, doctors diagnosed Mrs. Miller's condition. Shock. Mild concussion. Cuts and contusions. She was in no condition to swear out a complaint, let alone identify her assailant from a lineup.

Elmo was arraigned in Night Court. His brain began

working feverishly when he heard the arresting officer's charge. The old lady's deposition, taken at her bedside, claimed that there was an eyewitness. Some kid had seen the whole thing.

Elmo touched the empty place around his neck where the medal had hung. If that kid ever showed and put the finger on him, Elmo realized he could be put away for years. He knew who the little bastard was, the twerp he'd knocked over in the apartment-hotel elevator. I should have cut him then, when he fought back, Elmo thought.

With the court dockets jammed, with the cops unable to locate the alleged witness, moderate bail was set and a trial date postponed until Mrs. Miller was well enough to appear. A condition of Elmo's release was that he participate in a methadone program.

Elmo's one phone call was to his pusher who put up the bond money. As an investment. With Elmo into him for that much more, the pusher could put the screws on the dope-head to pull off a couple of *real* jobs just as soon as the heat was off.

Just when he was on the verge of really flipping out, Elmo was released from the Tombs. His relief slowly gave way to a mounting anger. "Me? Some kid get the best of me?" he swore. "Never!"

Elmo went immediately to the apartment-hotel looking for the little s.o.b., but he was nowhere in sight. After a couple of days of nosing around, Elmo learned the boy's name.

Nobody knew for sure where Jay-jay had gone. The wino-lady thought Ardis might have taken him along when she and her man had split to Florida for the winter. One neighbor claimed positively that the boy had moved upstate to live with blood relatives. Most of the people didn't give a damn. The kid was gone, that's all there was to it.

"But he's not gone!" Elmo muttered, as he hurried back to the park. He began to search the paths frantically. He located the bench where the kid had ambushed him. The bench with all sorts of writing on the slats.

Elmo bent down and examined it. "Their writing!" he exclaimed, recognizing Mrs. Miller's name from her deposition. Painstakingly, Elmo pieced the messages together. No matter which way he cut it, Elmo always came to the same conclusion: The kid was still around, somewhere. He hung out in the park a lot. So did the old lady. This bench was their meeting place.

"I'll stake out the whole area if I have to," Elmo said, clenching his jaws. "Sooner or later, he's going to show." Elmo's eyes swept over the landscape and came back to the bench. Goddamn! Didn't the old lady and the kid have a sweet little thing going on between them? That thought enraged Elmo all the more.

His shoulders hunched higher, the blood pounded in his temples until he thought his head would explode. Caught! For the first time in his life! And by a little kid!

Almost without his realizing it, the switchblade clicked open in Elmo's clenched fingers.

His fist swung through the air in a downward slash. "I'm—going—to—get—you!" he cried as the knife stabbed repeatedly into the bench slats. "I'm—going—to—get—you—good!"

Again and again the switchblade plunged into the wood, slashing and scarring until Elmo had obliterated all sense of the writing.

When he'd exhausted his rage. Elmo stared at the knife in his trembling hand. Better cool it, he thought, snapping the blade shut. *Got* to keep your cool. That's the only way you're going to get him.

"And I'm going to get you," Elmo whispered. "Before you have a chance to get me." The thought of laying his hands on him, fixing the little bastard for all the trouble he'd caused, became as compelling to Elmo as his habit.

If the kid is out of the way, he can never come to court and testify against me, then everything will go great for me again, Elmo thought.

And so day after day Elmo searched the park, his fingers endlessly telling the talismans on his string of rawhide. Only the medal was missing. But not for long.

Elmo trudged from the west side to the east, south and north, peering at the faces of every likely kid, working himself into a fever pitch as he traded one obsession for another.

PART THREE

Ten

The mugging had petrified Jay-jay and for three straight nights he dreamed of Elmo—Elmo's yellow eyes stalking him, Elmo's hands closing around his throat—then Jay-jay would wake up in a cold sweat.

"Elmo's in jail!" he chided himself. "You saw the cops handcuff him and drag him away."

If ever he was to get his castle built, Jay-jay knew he must push his fears aside. "Whatever's going to happen will happen soon enough without me worrying about it," he said, surveying the oak. "In the meantime, I've got to get something done."

Real good protection against the weather, that's what he needed. So far he'd been lucky, but this Indian summer wouldn't last forever. The leaves weren't as green as they'd been yesterday. They wouldn't be as green tomorrow. Someday it's going to snow! Jay-jay realized abruptly, and that somber thought made him put his butt in high gear.

They were always constructing something or repairing something in the park. Except above Ninety-sixth Street; here things were left pretty much as they fell. So the search for building materials took Jay-jay south.

On the way, he stopped off at a Comfort Station. Through the walls he could hear the voices of the attendants. He did his business and got out fast. Because a kid, alone, on a school day, at this hour? They'd grill him for sure. On the way out, Jay-jay unraveled some toilet paper, for future use. Leaves had been okay up to now, but with winter coming. . . .

Below the Ninety-seventh Street Transverse the thwack of tennis balls caught his ear. Beautiful people dressed in white volleyed back and forth. At the far end of the South Meadow workmen were leveling the terrain for new courts. Bulldozers grumbled and trees fell, poking their gnarled roots at the sky. Jay-jay strode past a stack of planks and lathing covered by a tarpaulin.

"Hmm, just the right size wood," he mused, the castle springing to shape. Remembering the tepee in the Museum of Natural History, Jay-jay realized that he could also make good use of the tarp. "But don't do anything in broad daylight," he warned his itchy fingers. "Come back after dark."

Heartened by the windfall of wood, Jay-jay skipped away. "Let's see what else is going on in the kingdom."

Directly ahead stretched a blue sea. A dusty jogging path followed the chain metal fence that enclosed the Reservoir. Jay-jay poked his nose through the fence and gazed at the ocean; it had to be an ocean because there were seagulls. A flotilla of canvasback ducks steamed by, the ducklings strung out in Indian file.

Jay-jay sidearmed a pebble through the fence. Beautiful to see the gulls beat their wings, faster, until they lifted from the water and soared into the sky only to dive and land and take off again when he skipped another stone. "If there's one wish I could have in the world," Jay-jay said, and, flinging out his arms, did a few loops in imitation of the white birds.

Jay-jay didn't harass the ducks, only the scavenger gulls. With colder weather, fewer people were coming into the park. "Meaning fewer leftovers," Jay-jay said as he hurled another rock. "The less competition the better."

Come to think of it, he hadn't seen that mutt around in a couple of days. The funny thing was, he almost missed him.

At this point, the Reservoir nearly filled the park's width. Jay-jay stared across the serene sea to the foreign land that was Fifth Avenue. Fat and shiny natives lived in the towers of that Oz, wrapped in furs and jewels, and they could have *anything* they wanted. Even as much spaghetti as they could eat.

Jay-jay clenched his fist. "Someday I'll sail across that sea, conquer that land and live like them!"

Then a wave of shame swept over him and he banged his head against the fence. "What does it matter how they live? Do they have branches for walls, birds for neighbors, the smell of things growing all around? And as soon as I locate tools and build my castle it's going to be the best home in the whole world!"

Around the south curve of the Reservoir Jay-jay jogged until he hit the Eighty-fifth Street Transverse. He continued east and almost bumped into the Twenty-second Police Precinct. He veered away *fast!* The Sheriff of Nottingham's men were everywhere! Jay-jay disappeared into the trees of Sherwood Forest just like he'd seen Robin Hood do on *The Best of Hollywood* on TV.

Cutting diagonally across the Great Lawn, Jay-jay approached the black monolith of Cleopatra's Needle. The obelisk, with carved hieroglyphics, speared its way toward the clouds.

Jay-jay read the inscription. "Built in 1500 b.c. Given to the people of the U.S. by the Egyptian government in friendship. 1881." He looked at it in wonder. Some guys had built this thing, let's see, three thousand, no three thousand five hundred years ago! And here it was.

The piercing buzz of an electric saw called to him and he headed toward Cedar Hill just south of the Seventy-ninth Street Transverse. Even before he got there his heart beat with sureness. This was where he'd find the tools!

A towering crane stood above the hill's crest. Cross girders and staircases and pulleys and winches and wheels grinding away. That was all he could see, for whatever else was going on was hidden by a twelve-foot-high wooden fence.

"Sounds like the CIA is digging clear through to China," Jay-jay said. But he couldn't count on guesses, no matter how educated. He had to *know*. Wrapping himself in his cloak of invisibility, Jay-jay went spying.

The closer he got to the top of Cedar Hill the less he could see. The fence ran around the site in irregular lines, like some kind of stockade. Not like Cowboys and Indians, those forts were square. This looked like King

Arthur's time, where the battlements followed the snaking of a river.

Warnings were plastered all over the fence: Danger! Blasting! Keep Away! Which only intensified Jay-jay's need to discover what was going on.

To soften the eyesore marring the gentle hill, friends of the park had painted magic marker flowers and inscriptions over the dull gray fence.

"We have met the enemy and he is us."

"Save the world, but start with the park."

"You live by dirt, you die by dirt."

"Old Japanese proverb: A man is a God in his own garden."

Jay-jay added a scarlet "Amen," and initialed it, T.P.O.C.P.

Around the fence he went to the East Drive. On an outcropping of mica rock, shaded by the magenta foliage of a spreading dogwood, a young couple were making love. They didn't see Jay-jay. Naturally, he was wearing his cloak of invisibility.

Turning another corner of the fence, Jay-jay happened on the main entrance of the construction camp. Tacked on the mammoth double doors, a notice explained it all.

To the Public

The construction of this site is part of the third city tunnel being built by the Board of Water Supply to deliver pure and wholesome water to the residents of N.Y.C. The new tunnel is needed to overcome serious deficiencies in the existing aqueduct system and to provide for future use. Every precaution is being observed to minimize inconvenience and. . . .

"Blah, blah, blah," Jay-jay finished. "What they really mean is New York is running out of water."

Now what you need is an aerial view of the insides, Jay-jay told himself. Figure out the lay of the land. Count of, what if you manage to sneak in there tonight and run into something you're not ready for?

Jay-jay continued following the fence, but it ended suddenly at the Seventy-ninth Street Transverse. The cut-stone retaining cliff bordering the roadbed formed a natural barrier on this side of the site.

"You've got two choices," Jay-jay muttered. "Give up, or—" He scrambled up on top of the wall. Extending his arms like balancing poles, he began to walk the ledge slowly. Traffic whizzed by below, buffeting him with intermittent blasts of air. Midway, the wall ended where the native rock jutted over the roadway. Pressing flat against the rocky face, Jay-jay inched forward. As he reached the point of no return he was overcome with dizziness. He shut his eyes and hung on until the spell passed.

A black cherry tree loomed just ahead at the point where the stone retaining wall ended and the wooden fence began again. Digging for a foothold on the embankment, Jay-jay stretched out and grabbed onto the tree trunk. Not daring to look down at the cars hurtling below, he eased himself around the overhang.

"Narrow escape," he breathed heavily. But it had given him access to the site, for the branches of the black cherry overhung the construction fence.

Jay-jay checked for counterspies, jumped up and caught the low limb. Chinning himself up, he very carefully crawled along the branch until he reached the fence.

His mouth fell open at the turmoil of the construction camp spreading before him. Right below, running alongside the Transverse retaining wall, an excavation was being blasted into the bedrock. A rickety wooden platform zigzagged around the rim of the hole to keep the workmen from falling into the pit. Seventy feet deep, at least! Jay-jay estimated.

A flexible yellow hose snaked into the muddy bottom drawing off the ground water. He got confused with all the equipment and the layout so he took out his pad and scribbled furiously, making a quick sketch.

Generators and pumps and a lot of machinery that Jay-jay didn't recognize. A bright red tractor labeled Lima. Stacks of oil drums and a sign, "No Smoking At Any Time."

Smoke rose from a rusty trash can where garbage was being burned. Hard hats swarmed everywhere, and there was a uniformed guard with a holster at his side. Parked near the main door was an aluminum trailer: Field Office Rental Service, A-Z Equipment Corporation. And a toolshed whose door was wide open!

Jay-jay watched the workers going in and out of the shed, carrying saws and drills and everything he needed.

"I knew this was the place," Jay-jay breathed, "I knew it!"

To one side of the toolshed stood an enormous empty wire spool, at least five feet in diameter. Jay-jay wished he could figure out a way to roll that home. He'd never want another toy for the rest of his life.

A yellow dump truck, an outhouse and, dominating everything, the dinosaur of the red derrick, its bucket teeth gnawing away at the excavation just below him.

Will this branch hold me if I go farther out? Jay-jay

wondered. Because he'd have to clear the fence and then drop onto the catwalk. Jay-jay gauged distances, telling himself it was possible. He imagined dropping toward the narrow ledge—missing—falling seventy feet into the pit—

"Too crazy dangerous!" shouted a frightened voice from his old life.

Dangerous it was, but this fortress contained everything he needed. Jay-jay folded the plan and put it in his pocket, still torn by do or don't.

"Tell you what," he said, swallowing hard, "if you can pick up the tools anyplace else, maybe at the tennis courts? Then you won't risk this place. Agreed? Agreed," he answered himself. "Leave it to fate."

It never occurred to Jay-jay, how, once inside, he would get out of the construction site.

Eleven

"Nothing I can do till dark," Jay-jay said. A light drizzle had begun to fall and the nearby Metropolitan Museum looked as good a place as any to kill a couple of hours. In the two times he'd been in them on school field trips, Jay-jay hadn't taken to this kind of museum. They were mostly about dead people and the things they owned.

"But at least it will be warm," he said, hopscotching along the orange and gray checkerboard squares that made up the sidewalk in front of the museum. Ranged along the top of the columned building, a row of stone ladies with seashell crowns regarded his approach.

Holding onto the gleaming brass banister, Jay-jay pulled himself up the twenty-eight steps to the museum's revolving doors and was swept into the Great Hall.

117

Shafts of light beamed down from three tremendous skylights. Arch upon arch supported the ceiling and Jay-jay whirled around, making the arches spin into circles.

On either side of the main entrance were hexagonal islands of banked plants surrounded by benches. Across the beige and salmon terrazzo floor Jay-jay slid, tingling with a sense of new worlds to explore.

"Jay-jay, cat burglar of the Met," he said under his breath. "But I bet all their tools would be antiques."

"Students Admitted Free," the sign read. Jay-jay hitched up his dungarees and sauntered past the zombie guard. Even though I'm not in school anymore, I'm not lying, he thought, on account of I'm a student of *life*. And he giggled aloud.

Rain had made it an off-day and Jay-jay practically had the museum to himself. Every room was like a time machine, transporting him back to old worlds. He inspected the black vase with orange figures on it that had set the museum back a million dollars. So the acquisitions brochure said proudly. In another room filled with paintings, Jay-jay contemplated *Aristotle Contemplating the Bust of Homer.*

A creaky lady and a man who looked like a limp asparagus crowded Jay-jay's view.

"Absolutely brilliant," the dowager said. "And to think that the museum got it for a *song.* Only four million."

"Brilliant, absolutely," the man said.

Jay-jay decided that he wouldn't have shelled out four million, not for that. Imagine all the trees and flowers he could have planted instead?

In the Indian Art Hall, Jay-jay came across a statue

titled *The Amorous Couple*. He circled them with a keen eye and growing interest. The lady had one leg thrown over her lover and the man—

You can learn a lot in a place like this, Jay-jay realized, with a whole new respect for museums. Like folks were even doing it way back in the thirteenth century, Ganga Dynasty. And standing up!

After he'd exhausted his fantasies, Jay-jay moved on to the next statue. *Buddha*, Tanjore Region, Chola Dynasty. Late ninth, early tenth century. This dude had four faces, each looking in a different direction.

So he can spot whoever's coming, Jay-jay figured, with an oblique recollection of Elmo. You think maybe if we really knew each other we might be friends? Jay-jay asked himself. Then he sighed and shrugged. Nope, like cats and dogs.

Some good-luck freak had put a shiny penny into Buddha's palm. Jay-jay checked the room, saw nobody was watching and plucked the penny from the fingers.

For the next hour Jay-jay plunged himself into the Medieval Hall. Here was something he could understand! In the Equestrian Court, knights in armor were ranged along the walls. Right down the center of the court, six knights marched along on horseback. The front leg of each horse was raised so it looked like they were about to take a step. Heraldic banners flew from the surrounding wooden balconies. Jay-jay shut his eyes and heard the flourish of trumpets and the crash of mace and sword.

Then Jay-jay came upon a tapestry that made him stop cold in his tracks. On loan from the Cloisters, the plaque said. *The Hunting of the Unicorn*.

A hundred ladies must have sewed for a hundred years

to make something like this, Jay-jay thought, his hungry gaze sweeping across the wall hanging.

Through a dense forest of russet and greens galloped the hunters, bows drawn, lances pointed. Their white horses plunged and swelled, men and maidens ran after, beating the bush. The unicorn fled and bled in the formal woven forest as he'd done for seven hundred years.

Jay-jay's hand moved impulsively toward the fabled creature. His arm wavered then and dropped to his side. The unicorn ran on, as it would run forever.

And suddenly Jay-jay realized what museums were all about. Not dead people or the things they owned. It was a way of stopping time. Even though somebody had died hundreds of years ago they were saying, "Look! Remember me for the beautiful thing I made!"

Before leaving the second floor, Jay-jay went back to the Indian Section and put the penny back in Buddha's palm.

"Not that I believe in any of *your* superstitions," he said to the benign smiling face, "but I've got a big night ahead of me and I'll need all the luck I can get. Besides, what can you buy for a penny nowadays?"

Down twenty-three steps to the first landing of the Great Staircase, twenty-three more down to the main floor.

"Am I going nuts?" Jay-jay said as his sniffing nostrils picked up the scent of food. He followed the aroma through the Greek and Roman Halls where snickering girls sneaked glances at the naked statues. Then down a long vaulted hallway—his nose hadn't led him astray! There at the end of the museum was a big fancy cafeteria.

"One Dollar Minimum," Jay-jay read, and pulling out

his empty pockets said, "it might as well be a thousand."

The entire cafeteria was painted black and the arched ceiling was lit with concealed fluorescent lighting. Taking up the middle of the floor was a huge pool surrounded by tall white columns and lots of potted palms. Three bronze dolphins were about to leap out of the water and seven naked bronze people were riding other porpoises. Streams of water fountained out of the dolphins' blowholes. But if you looked real fast, Jay-jay decided, then it seemed like the dolphins were leaping through hoops of water.

Dining tables were ranged around the pool. Jay-jay nearly flipped out at the sight of busboys carrying away trays of dishes. The busboys all looked like oversized puppets in their pale blue velvet jackets, black pants and big blue bowties.

And then Jay-jay saw the good luck that Buddha had bought him. Glinting in the refracted waters of the pool there must have been ten thousand pennies! Even some nickels and dimes! Thrown into the water by people making wishes.

Jay-jay didn't hesitate a second. He kicked off his sneakers, knotted the laces and hung his shoes around his neck. Tennis courts or Cedar Hill, whichever fate decided, the thing that would make his foray a success was a full meal!

A glittering middle-aged woman wrapped in sealskin watched Jay-jay with bored detachment. But her mouth fell open when he jumped into the pool.

"It's not even up to my knees," Jay-jay said, as he started collecting. In short order he scooped up more than twenty-five pennies. Then he stopped counting and concentrated on a mother lode of dimes and quarters.

The diners at poolside stood up and pointed and laughed. Jay-jay paid no attention to the applause, his arms moved like a reaper gathering the coins.

A museum guard, drawn by the commotion rushed into the restaurant. "Get the hell out of there!" he waved to the boy.

Jay-jay worked faster.

The guard yelled to a grinning busboy. "Get him out of there! Hear? Go in and get him!"

"Get him youself," the busboy shot back.

Jay-jay ducked under the spewing fountains, scrambled out the far side of the pool and fled, leaving a trail of footprints along the marble floors. In a twinkling he'd reached an exit and was safely outside, the coins jingling merrily in his pockets.

The $2.22 he'd collected bought him a bowl of vegetable soup, and a steaming plate of spaghetti and meatballs at the Zoo Cafeteria. He would have preferred eating at the elegant museum cafeteria, but under the circumstances. . . .

After a last swing around the cages to say good night, Jay-jay started home. And back to the tennis courts, he realized, hiccuping from food and nerves. Which would it be?

The racing clouds were limned by the sun's last light, fanning an eerie blue haze over the land. Dusk touched the park lamps and they blinked on, holding the deepening haze a moment longer.

The tennis courts were deserted, not even a watchman. The planks of wood were lying where he'd seen them. But there were no tools anywhere, not a hammer, a nail, nothing.

An ominous feeling came over Jay-jay. Now that fate had decided, he wasn't so sure.

Jay-jay helped himself to as many planks as he could carry, which turned out to be two at a time. He lugged the first haul back to the tree and made four more trips. On the fifth go-round, Jay-jay took the tarpaulin and a dozen strips of lathing. He secreted the wood in a hollow not far from his oak.

Jay-jay sensed that the Cedar Hill job would be tough, much tougher than the grammar school. After all, he'd known that territory. Somehow, he felt he was being tested. One thing to *say* that you wanted a new life.

"But what a whole different bag it is to make it happen," Jay-jay said ruefully.

Up into the oak Jay-jay climbed, to rest and prepare himself. He studied the map until it was too dark to see. Am I seeing better or worse since I broke my glasses? he wondered, rubbing his eyes.

He cinched his safety line around the tree trunk with a double half-hitch. "If I pull this off tonight, then this is the last time I'll have to tie myself up like this."

Jay-jay tried to nap, but every time he dozed off he was aware of relentless yellow eyes stalking him, eyes that were not those of a friend. Nor could he get the scarred and mutilated bench out of his mind.

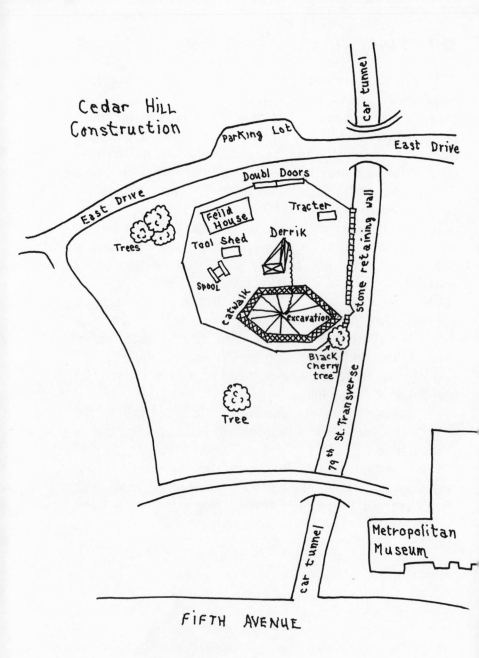

Cedar Hill
Construction

Parking Lot

car tunnel

East Drive

East Drive

Doubl Doors

Tracter

Feild House

Trees

Tool Shed

Derrik

Spool

catwalk

excavation

Black Cherry tree

Stone retaining wall

Tree

79th St. Transverse

car tunnel

Metropolitan Museum

FIFTH AVENUE

Twelve

Jay-jay woke with a groan; the cord had jerked into his ribs when he turned. The elusive moonlight filtered through the leaves silvering everything it touched.

"What time is it?" he wondered sleepily.

Then the howl of a distant dog told him it was the hour of the wolf; between three and four o'clock, he figured, remembering a *Creature Feature*. The dark time before dawn when the grim reaper waited to snatch unsuspecting souls.

"Do it tomorrow," Jay-jay told himself, and answered, "If you don't do it tonight you'll never get up the nerve again."

Slipping out of his body noose, Jay-jay slung the canvas bag around his shoulders and climbed down to the ground.   Moonlight couldn't penetrate through the thick covering and it took awhile before he got accustomed to the dark.

"Avoid the paths, avoid the paths," came the message with each heartbeat. That's where the police cars prowled and if they spotted him it would be all over.

"So I'm just not going to let them spot me," he whispered.

A broken ribbon of light carved into the park at the Ninety-seventh Street Transverse. The west end of the road had only one pedestrian overpass. Jay-jay waited until there was no traffic and then dashed across the bridge. "Bad spot there," he told himself. "Easy to be trapped."

The Reservoir was even more dangerous. For maybe a quarter of a mile Jay-jay would be paralleling the roadway of the West Drive, the road the police used on their sentry rounds. There was no other way; he started around.

The moon came from behind its cloud cover and peeled the darkness from the waters. Gulls and ducks huddled in clumps and Jay-jay threw no stones this time. He had just reached the narrowest strip of land at Eighty-eighth Street when Jay-jay saw the patrol car swing off the road and move in his direction. He dove for the nearest cover. The crunch of tires on gravel came closer, stopped.

Then a gruff voice, "Probably your imagination. The light can play tricks on you."

"I tell you I saw something," the other cop said.

Two of them, like on *Adam-12*, Jay-jay thought. He heard the car door open. The beam of a flashlight stabbed in all directions, sweeping over the very bushes where he lay. Jay-jay held his breath, absolutely sure that his heart was beating loud enough to be heard in the nearest precinct.

A squawk on the car radio broke the stillness. Then the voice of the second cop calling to his partner, "Let's move it. Some left-over hippies are streaking around in the Sheep Meadow."

The footsteps drew away from Jay-jay. He watched the twin white beams turn to twin reds as the car gunned into the darkness. He waited until everything was quiet before he broke cover.

Soon the expanse of the Great Lawn lay before him and Jay-jay decided to chance crossing it. "Nobody's going to pick you out in all that space," he said. He continued talking to keep his courage up. "And there's no road here for cops to come pestering people."

Dawn couldn't be too far off. An hour and a half at the most; this job had to be finished before daylight! On Jay-jay's left loomed the dark presence of the Met. To the south, high on its battlements, rose Belvedere Castle. The towers looked ghostly in the retreating moonlight and the twin spire in Belvedere Lake rippled and then vanished before a sorcerer's dark wind.

"Glad I've got no business there tonight," Jay-jay said, shuddering. When he crossed the bridge over the Seventy-ninth Street Transverse at the East Drive his heart sank.

The Cedar Hill construction site was lit up as bright as a night ball game! "Why didn't I figure on floodlights?" He spat and punched his thigh. "Because you're dumb, that's why. You just don't have any luck!"

Jay-jay's shoulders slumped. On the verge of turning

back he remembered the moment in the oak when he'd
sworn that he would be his own good luck. Straightening
up, he took a couple of deep breaths. "Don't let a stupid
thing like a few searchlights stop you. Fact, they'll make
it easier to see what you're doing."

Keeping to the underbrush, Jay-jay swung round to
the Transverse side of the site. Very carefully, he began
to walk the stone ledge of the retaining wall. The
dinosaur tower poked its head over the wooden fence,
keeping its searchlight eye on Jay-jay wherever he went.
There was the black cherry tree and in a few seconds
Jay-jay was up in its branches.

Below, the compound lay in harsh light and shadow.
Exactly like he'd memorized it from his plan. Except
now the catwalk fringing the deep pit looked about a
half-inch wide.

Jay-jay wiped the sweat from his forehead, then
crawled out on the limb until he was just over the fence.
The catwalk was about fifteen feet below. Beyond that,
stretched the yawning darkness of the pit.

"Some fly up to heaven, others fall—" Jay-jay began,
suddenly remembering that sermon. "Don't even think
of that!" he commanded himself.

Moving with infinite care, Jay-jay straddled the fence.
He swung his leg over the inside, grabbed the top of the
fence and slowly lowered himself until he was hanging
by his fingertips. He had shortened the drop. Only about
eight feet now.

Hanging there, Jay-jay suddenly realized that once
inside, he didn't have any way of getting out! "I don't
want to do this," he grunted. "I want to go home!"

But he didn't have the strength to chin himself back
up. Jay-jay took a deep breath—it might be his last—and

let go. The pain shot up his legs as he hit. The catwalk shuddered under the impact of his weight, but held.

He flattened against the catwalk planking. Nothing stirred in the compound. "See? I told you you'd make your own luck! . . . Some luck! I'm trapped in here forever."

Wishing that the floodlights weren't so relentless, Jay-jay crawled around the perimeter of the excavation until he got to solid ground. He darted to the yellow dump truck, crawled under the wheels to the other side. Waited, dashed to the red tower and hid behind the steel girders. All he wanted to do was get out! He was so scared that he had to pee. When the moon disappeared behind a cloud, Jay-jay stole across the clearing to the A-Z field house.

Jay-jay peered in through the lighted window. The guard lay dozing on a cot. From the look of his white hair he was pretty old; that was good. He had a pistol strapped to his waist; that was bad.

Jay-jay looked around wildly for a way to escape. And then he saw it. The main gate was bolted from the inside by a simple crossbar. All he had to do was lift the crossbar and slip out the double doors. A couple of seconds' head start and he'd be lost in the dark.

Calmed somewhat, Jay-jay decided to go through with the original plan. He backed off from the trailer and made it to the toolshed. No lock on the door, but it creaked as he pushed it open. Pitch black inside. But then the moon decided to help. Emerging from its cloud cover, it stabbed through the panes, painting a brilliant moon-window on the floor of the shack.

There it all was, neatly hung on pegboard. Jay-jay moved quickly, dumping one of each tool into his canvas bag. Medium-size hammer; a saw; a screwdriver; handfuls of nails and screws. He spied a large coil of clothesline rope on the workbench and stuffed the entire thing into his knapsack.

The slam of a door made him freeze. Through the window, Jay-jay saw the watchman come out of his trailer and start his rounds. Too late to slip out the toolshed door, the guard was heading right his way. Searching frantically for a place to hide, Jay-jay jammed himself behind a bin full of woodshavings.

The watchman approached the toolshed. Saw the open door. Scratched his head. "Queer," the guard said. He distinctly remembered closing the shed at quitting time. He went inside and switched on the light. Empty.

He shrugged and went out again. Then he walked to the main doors and checked them. Still locked from the inside. He leaned against the crossbar and lit a cigar.

Jay-jay stuck his head above the woodbin and peeped out the window. Damnation! The guard looked like he'd settled against the main doors for the rest of the night!

And that's my only way out, Jay-jay thought desperately. I'll never be able to climb that fence with this bag, it weighs a ton. Nope, it was the double doors or nothing.

Lucky for Jay-jay, the toolshed door was not in the watchman's line of vision, and he crept outside. So far so good. Champing at the bit, he waited another couple of minutes, *willing* the watchman to leave the gates.

"Only for a second," Jay-jay prayed. "That's all I'll need, only a second."

But the guard didn't move and with daylight just freedom's breath away Jay-jay knew that more than prayers were necessary. Something drastic had to be done.

The toolshed was built on the slant of the hill. A few feet from where Jay-jay lay hidden, stood the gigantic wooden spool, empty of wire. He elbowed his way across the ground to the spool. Two wooden chocks kept it from rolling and Jay-jay pulled them away. He leaned his shoulder against the spool and pushed. But the contraption was too heavy.

Getting on his back, Jay-jay braced his feet against the two wheels and shoved with all his might. Slowly, ever so slowly, the spool began to roll, a little faster now, gathering momentum as it picked up speed down the hill.

The guard caught sight of the spool just as it hurtled past the derrick. He started running after it even as it careened off a garbage can and headed straight for the catwalk surrounding the excavation pit.

The spool sailed over the edge, was lost from sight for a second, and then came the fearful sound of splintering wood as it smashed on the rocks below.

The watchman leaned over the edge of the pit and stared down at the wreckage.

Jay-jay used this moment to run madly for the main gate.

The guard turned just as Jay-jay got to the double doors. The watchman couldn't believe his eyes. Some midget was stealing the equipment! He fumbled with the snap on his holster and drew his gun.

Jay-jay yanked at the wooden crossbar holding the doors shut. But try as he strength. he was too short to get the right leverage. The guard came puffing up the hill.

"Stop or I'll shoot!"

Jay-jay wet his pants. With a last desperate effort he pushed the bar with all his strength. The doors swung open and Jay-jay disappeared into a stand of spruce just as the gun went off high over his head.

With his knapsack full of tools clanking, and stumbling over himself, Jay-jay crashed through the grove, running a broken-field course. Not daring to risk the openness of the Great Lawn, when Jay-jay ran across the Seventy-ninth Street Transverse bridge he cut sharp left to the heavy woods leading to Belvedere Castle.

Run, that's all he could think of, paying no attention to the pain that burned his lungs, sprinting past Belvedere Lake and dropping exhausted in the Shakespeare Garden.

He lay in the bushes panting, wanting only to flake out right then and there. But in fifteen minutes at most it would get light. And you couldn't trust those crazy joggers, Jay-jay thought; some of them were up and running with the dawn.

The scream of a police siren pried Jay-jay to his feet. He started running again, this time following the bridle path north. Great stretches of it were shielded from sight by bushes and trees.

Jay-jay wasn't exactly sure of how long it took him to get back to the oak. He must have stopped a half dozen times to hide from the police cars tearing by. When he got to the squeeze of the Reservoir he gave up being cautious and just ran. As luck would have it, all the patrol cars had been dispatched to Cedar Hill, so none were cruising around the Reservoir.

At last Jay-jay reached home. He pressed his face against the rough bark. "I've never been so happy to be anywhere in my life," he said, gulping for air. After a bit, he cached his tools in the same hollow where he'd hidden the planks of wood.

With his flagging strength he climbed into the thick branches. He tried to drop off to sleep, but he was so charged up he couldn't. His stomach rumbled up a complaint that made his head reel. Was his fate always to be hungry?

"If I managed to get wood and tools, then why can't I do the same about food?" Jay-jay demanded. There was something so ugly about scrounging stuff from garbage cans. "And you won't even have that source once it gets really cold. Think of something!" he said, kneading his stomach.

But exhaustion got the better of him and Jay-jay curled into the crook of the branches. Outside of his nagging fear about food, he was so happy with the way the night had turned out that he couldn't understand why he cried until he fell asleep.

Thirteen

From her bed on the eleventh floor of Flower Fifth Hospital, Mrs. Miller looked across the avenue to the Conservatory Gardens of Central Park, and beyond to the rolling meadows and wild hills.

Is he hungry? she wondered.

Mrs. Miller had told the authorities about her prince who lived in the park. She felt she had to protect him, help him. The policemen and the doctors had listened and nodded, but the minute her back was turned Mrs. Miller knew they were making fun of her. Well, she was going home in a few days, that's what an intern had told her and she would take care of him herself. She knitted another line of the scarf, his scarf.

Going home also meant that she would have to testify against that hoodlum. She was terrified of that, but what else could she do?

135

"You just can't let them run around like crazy animals," she said to the nurse, who had just come in with the thermometer. Mrs. Miller had told the entire nursing staff the whole story the day they brought her in.

The nurse nodded as she checked Mrs. Miller's pulse. An unusual case, the nurse mused. The woman didn't look senile and her vital functions were normal. Maybe that nasty crack on the head had tipped her in that direction. A prince indeed, the nurse thought, moving to the next patient. There weren't any in real life, let alone living in Central Park.

The steam began to rattle in the radiator pipes, and Mrs. Miller wondered, Is he cold? She hoped that this Indian summer would linger on, at least until she was well enough to search him out. Bring him some hot food and warm clothes. Or maybe . . . he would even listen to her proposition?

Dreaming of the castle turned out to be easier than building it. "First thing," Jay-jay said, "I've got to get all the equipment into the tree."

It turned out to be a labor that would have confounded Hercules and almost cost Jay-jay his life.

Leaves crackled underfoot as he went to his secret cache and dug up everything he had liberated from the tennis courts and Cedar Hill. Jay-jay worked as fast as he could, aware that at any moment somebody hiking in the area might discover him. Bird-watchers, you really had to watch out for those kooks.

At last Jay-jay had everything at the base of the oak. He unfolded the tarp and carefully stacked the planks and tools in it. Spaced along the edges of the canvas were steel-grommet holes. He cut a length of rope from his coil and wove it through the holes, tying both ends of the tarp together. It made sort of a sling-cradle.

Jay-jay cut off another length of rope, very long this time, tied one end securely to the sling-tarp and made a lasso with the other end of the rope. He slipped the lasso over his head and drew it tight around his chest and under his arms. He'd purposely left about three feet of free rope hanging from the chest harness end, in case he had to anchor himself to rest as he climbed into the tree.

By now the flat disk of the November sun had circled into mid-heaven. Jay-jay was perspiring and his stomach gurgled like mad. But he warned himself that if he took time to rest he'd never finish. Last night he'd seen his breath frost in the air. "And it's going to get colder tonight," he said. "And one day it's going to snow! Jesus!"

He patted his complaining stomach. "Bear with me a little longer, huh?"

Trailing the rope behind him like the golden umbilical cord of the astronauts, Jay-jay started to climb up the oak. Getting to the first limb had always been a bitch. "Whatever happened to your plan to invent an easier way of getting up and down?" he panted. "Your brain is going to die on you if you don't start using it, lazy bones."

Winded, Jay-jay finally made it to the spot where he'd decided to build. The rope snaked down from his chest harness to the bundle of building materials still on the ground.

Many reasons had gone into his choice of location. For one, it was high enough from the ground so it couldn't be seen. Two, the series of thick branches growing from the trunk would make perfect anchoring points for the floor.

The third reason, and not the least, was there was a window through the boughs that looked clear up to the sky. In some corner of his heart, Jay-jay had never given up his dream of one day being able to fly.

Bracing himself on the branch, Jay-jay gripped the rope and slowly began to haul the tarp up. He didn't need more than one tug to realize that he'd never do it. The load was so heavy that every time he pulled he lost his footing.

He fought against the despair slowly filling him. Racking his brain, Jay-jay thought of every book he'd ever read, every TV show, every droning word of his science teacher explaining the principles of levers and pulleys and physics. "Why didn't I pay more attention!" he chastised himself.

A germ of an idea blossomed, slowly at first, but then growing with bean stalk speed until Jay-jay was electric with excitement.

"It's tricky," he said, with a swift glance at the ground. But that very fact seemed to spur him on. Heart thudding, Jay-jay climbed up to a higher limb and looped the rope over the branch. He jumped up and down on the limb to make sure it would support his weight.

"Let's see, I weigh eighty-nine pounds. Or at least I did when I first came to live here. The loaded tarp must weigh maybe thirty pounds." He checked and double-checked. "Your calculations better be right or this is the last physics problem you'll ever try to solve."

Adam's apple quivering, Jay-jay began the count-down. "Ten, nine, eight, seven, six, five, four, three, two, one—" and stepped off into space.

His being leaped with the thrill of the fall. This was the closest he'd ever come to flying! He yelled, "We have a lift-off!"

Jay-jay fell six feet before the slack was used up and now he was bobbing at the end of the line. The chest harness dug into his armpits, and he bit his lip to keep from crying out. The rope was waxed so there was little friction as it looped over the limb. Jay-jay dangled for a moment, and then those laws his instructor had mumbled about took over. Gravity did. the rest, and Jay-jay continued down at a reasonably slow pace.

As Jay-jay descended, the tarp started up. He watched it approach him, reached out and touched it as it passed and was unable to stifle a yowl of joy.

Docking procedure was going to be perfect! Jay-jay realized as he looked up. The tarp would come to rest about a foot from where he intended to build. "How's that for on target!" he said.

Then all at once, catastrophe! The tarp-cradle got stuck in a tangle of branches, leaving Jay-jay dangling in midair. He strained his arms upward, but the payload was just out of reach. Jerking on the line, Jay-jay bounced up and down, trying to dislodge the materials, but he only managed to wedge it tighter.

A hundred years from now, Jay-jay thought, somebody will find a skeleton hanging in this tree and they'll wonder how it happened! Jay-jay might have had a good laugh on himself if his predicament wasn't so serious. He flailed about, growing more panicky by the second.

There was only one alternative left. To his right, a branch extended, also just out of reach. Using his body as a pendulum, Jay-jay started to swing, increasing the arc until his toes touched the limb. Another swing and he almost had his ankles around it. And then with a final effort, Jay-jay sailed at it again and scissored his legs around the branch.

"So far, so good," he grunted, hanging on for dear

life. Then, taking the free end of the rope from his chest harness, Jay-jay tied that to the branch he was straddling. Squirming and pulling, Jay-jay fought his way out of the body noose and hauled himself onto a limb. The tarp-cradle remained stuck in the branches.

Free of his burden, Jay-jay felt as if he were going to float away. But his relief and success had made him careless and when he started to unload the tarp, he slipped and fell from his perch.

With a lunge born of desperation, Jay-jay grabbed a fistful of twigs. It broke his fall enough for him to catch a lower, sturdier limb. Jay-jay squeezed the branch to his body while the ground below revolved in his swimming vision.

"So close!" Jay-jay whispered.

But the fall had taught him something. There was a time to build and a time to rest. He shook his head and said, "So better put off till tomorrow what will kill you today."

Fourteen

The following morning, Jay-jay woke up furious with himself. "If you'd had something decent to eat before you started to build, you wouldn't have fallen," he said, and started out, determined to discover a new source of food.

His scavenging route took him very far south this time, all the way to the garbage cans of the Tavern on the Green. He teased his hunger by gnawing at a ham bone. An anger was growing in Jay-jay, an anger about being hungry all the time. While those people sitting in the Tavern's picture window spent their time stuffing their faces.

Two ladies came out of the restaurant and their voices carried to Jay-jay. One lady said, "I was a *very* bad girl today, Sylvie, but tomorrow I'm definitely starting on my diet."

"That's what's so wonderful about life, Ceil," the other lady answered, "there's always another tomorrow."

Jay-jay watched them get into a cab and drive off. "Will I ever be able to eat in a fancy place like that? Someday I'll figure out a way. And when I do? Watch out, world!"

Starting back for home, Jay-jay came upon the wonder of the Adventure Playground at Sixty-seventh Street. A sign lured him in with the invitation to:

ENJOY

run. hop. skip. jump. litter.

skate. leap. laugh. giggle.

wiggle. jog. romp. swing. slide.

frolic. climb. bicycle. stretch.

read. relax. imbibe. play. sleep.

"Why not?" Jay-jay shrugged. Slide, frolic and climb took him to the stepped pyramid of an Aztec temple. Jay-jay charged up the steps to the sacrificial peak, bared his heart to the sun and plummeted down the sliding pond to the sand pit.

Just then, a platoon of children wearing the blue and white uniforms of a local private school, filed into the playground. They marched in twos to the low concrete amphitheater and took seats.

"Like a lot of robots," Jay-jay muttered. "And not a lunch box in the whole bunch."

A willowy teacher-lady with a flowered scarf and flowing gestures clapped her hands for attention. She opened a story book and began to act out the weekly installment.

Jay-jay crawled out of the sandbox and edged nearer.

The teacher said, "And then Robinson Crusoe came upon footprints in the sand and was struck with fear. Were there savages on this desert isle who wanted to kill him?"

"Eat him, probably," Jay-jay mumbled.

Flower lady stopped and looked at Jay-jay inquisitively, inviting him to join her group. There was nothing Jay-jay liked better than finding out how a good story ended, but at that moment he had to put those childhood pleasures behind him. For he had just spied a jungle gym made out of rough hewn telephone poles and iron cross bars. From the topmost rung a long rope hung down with knots in it every foot or so.

Jay-jay sprang to his feet. "Now why didn't I think of that?" The *perfect* way to get in and out of my oak, especially since I still have lots of rope left from the Cedar Hill rip-off—uh, liberation, he corrected himself.

"Maybe this is what living's all about?" Jay-jay reasoned. "Even when you've been knocked for a loop, if you keep your eyes and ears open, sooner or later the way to solve your problem shows up. Providing you don't die of starvation first."

"I wonder if things look different when you're not hungry?" Jay-jay said, browsing selectively through the wire trash cans along the route to home. Twice he hit the jackpot, the carcass of a chicken, half a loaf of stale Italian bread. Finally, he had scavenged a good enough haul to keep him until he finished building his home.

"Someday, *I'll* throw things in garbage cans," Jay-jay said resolutely.

Peeking above the treetops at Eightieth Street, he

could see the round dome of the Planetarium. This time he caught the afternoon show.

Jay-jay took a seat in the auditorium with the rest of the crowd. The lights gradually dimmed until it was night and the stars began to wink in the curve of the dome. He listened intently as the lecturer explained about the planets and hot stars and cold stars and the possibility of life on other worlds. Then a simulated blast-off and a lunar orbit and then back to Earth and all too quickly the lights went on.

After the Planetarium show Jay-jay continued home. He stumbled across a treasure in a clump of bushes at the foot of Summit Rock. Tossed away by some affluent hippies, by the look of the embroidery and patches.

"A sleeping bag!" Jay-jay whispered, crushing it close to his chest. He glanced around furtively, lest the owner appear and snatch away this piece of good fortune.

A quick inspection revealed that the foot-end of the bag had ripped; some of the fiberglass insulation was sticking out. But nothing that he couldn't eventually fix. "Especially if I can get my hands on needle and thread. Maybe Mrs. Miller—?" Jay-jay broke off suddenly depressed. He hadn't seen her in a long time. Was she all right? Had Elmo hurt her bad? Elmo. Even though he was safe in jail, Jay-jay couldn't get him out of his mind.

Early the next morning, Jay-jay set to work. Making the ladder was easy enough. He straddled the lowest limb of the oak, unraveled the rope from the coil, tying heavy knots in it every twelve inches. "That's what I'll use for footholds." He continued tying knots until the length of rope reached the ground.

But figuring out a way to hide the ladder? That was

something else again. He just couldn't leave it there, or anybody could climb up. Jay-jay sat there, legs dangling, thinking until his behind began to ache. Then he bounced with the solution.

"All you've got to do is *double* the length of rope!" he told himself excitedly. "And now loop the two strands over the branch."

The two free ends of the rope hung down to the grass. Twining his legs around the rope, but making sure to hold onto both strands, Jay-jay lowered himself to the ground. "And to think I couldn't climb the ropes in gym class!"

As soon as his feet touched the earth, Jay-jay yanked one end of the rope, pulling the whole contraption down to him. "Solved! Whenever I leave the tree, I hide the ladder in my secret place," Jay-jay said. "Then when I come back home, all I do is dig it up." At that moment, not even the guy who'd dreamed the Brooklyn Bridge could have been as proud as Jay-jay.

A whimper from the bush put Jay-jay instantly on the alert. Crawling through the shrubbery came—damn! That hound again. Jay-jay picked up a stick, mayhem on his mind. The mutt cowered and looked at him with liquid, helpless eyes. Jay-jay realized then that the dog was plenty sick.

"Distemper, probably, that's what the ranger called it on *Lassie*," Jay-jay remembered. He said to the pup, "Well, we've got two choices. I can carry you to a far-off part of the park and let you drift up to dog heaven. Or—oh, what the hell!" Jay-jay picked up the animal and give or take a paw or two, managed to tuck him into his shirt. The pup felt burning hot against Jay-jay's ribs.

"Good thing I invented this ladder or I could have

never carried you up," Jay-jay said. He rolled up an end of the rope and hurled it over the lowest limb. Evening the ends, he grasped both strands firmly and hand over hand pulled himself up, using the knots as resting places for his feet.

Once on the branch, Jay-jay lifted the ladder out of sight. He climbed higher into the oak and stowed the coiled ladder in the sling-tarp which was still wedged in the crook of the branches. Next, Jay-jay slipped two planks of wood out of the tarpaulin and laid them across the branches.

"So that we'll have a place to lie down. It would have been easier if you showed up *after* I finished building, but I guess that's never the way."

He took the pup out of his shirt and set him on the planks. "What shall I call you?" Jay-jay asked. "You're a funny-looking thing. White and black and brown and marmalade. A Heinz dog, fifty-seven varieties. How about . . . Rainbow? Nah, that doesn't give you a chance to be sad. Simon and Garfunkel? No? Let's see, you're always so nervous and jerky, what about if I call you—Tomorrow? Or I could call you Friday. Nope, that's not original, and you're definitely an original. I know! The way you're always tagging after me? I'll call you Shadow!"

Jay-jay unzipped the sleeping bag. The pup wagged his tail feebly as Jay-jay tucked him in.

"Shadow it is, then," Jay-jay said, nuzzling him.

The rest of the day Jay-jay tended to the pup as best he could, bringing him water and scraps. With darkness the pup seemed to get worse. Hours passed, Against the midnight heavens, the sky shifted in patterns of deep grays and blues.

Jay-jay stared up through the window. "Shadow, if you make believe the clouds are standing still, then it's us that's moving through the sky."

About one o'clock the clouds massed with the heaviness of autumn, jamming against each other as a storm gathered momentum. "Just what we needed," Jay-jay said, and working furiously, squirmed into the sleeping bag alongside Shadow. "Now don't move," he told the dog, "because the planks aren't fastened down yet."

Everything in the air forecast rain, the energy that crackled all about, the flashes of lightning, the distant rumble that grew more ominous as the storm swept toward the city.

"Think we'd be safer on the ground?" Jay-jay asked Shadow. "Probably, but that would be like deserting a friend."

The storm hit about three o'clock. A bolt of lightning startled Jay-jay from his half sleep. He watched the sky crack again and again. "Boy, you're not kidding around up there, are you?" he whispered.

The rain fell then, battering the leaves and lashing the branches in a mournful fury. For the first few minutes Jay-jay went through a delicious terror. "Nothing to be scared of," he said, hugging Shadow as the rain beat against the oak, then found its way down to the sleeping bag. "We're dry and safe in here."

Shadow whined feebly. Jay-jay opened his shirt and held him close against his body to keep him warm, and it seemed that his strength was flowing into the limp and scruffy pup.

Soon the water began to beat against the sleeping bag. Jay-jay kept his nose poked out the zippered covering.

The branches had turned darker against the assault of rain. All around them lightning played, flashing blue and white.

Suddenly there was a fearful crash. A bolt struck the nearby elm and nearly sliced it in half. Jay-jay pressed his ears to drown out the ringing noise. He clutched Shadow, telling him not to be frightened, that everything was going to be all right.

As the storm grew in intensity Jay-jay became aware of a strange new feeling. Something he'd never known before, something that made him feel like a giant. The more warmth and strength he gave to Shadow, the stronger and warmer, he, Jay-jay seemed to become.

Hour after hour Jay-jay clung to his perch, alternately yelling back at the storm and praying. At dawn it ended abruptly. But a new crisis developed.

Shadow twitched helplessly in the throes of a convulsion. His back feet moved independently of the rest of his body. Then he stopped thrashing and lay still and Jay-jay thought that he had died. Tears welled to Jay-jay's eyes as he stroked the dog.

"I could have been nicer to you. I should have! But now it's too late!"

But no, there was the faint rise and fall of Shadow's rib cage! Jay-jay pressed his face to Shadow's. Even his nose didn't feel hot anymore!

Shadow's tail thumped once against Jay-jay's chest. Only then did Jay-jay manage to doze off, a tight, tired smile on his lips.

When he woke, Jay-jay surveyed the damage. He'd have guessed that the city would be washed away. But there was the skyline, stony as ever.

The real wonder was the tree. Some weaker branches had crashed to the ground, true. But the rest of it . . . the remaining leaves looked like they'd been freshly polished. Everything smelled new, as though the oak had gathered energy from the storm and had changed it into some kind of growth.

Jay-jay reached out and put one hand against the trunk and the other hand on Shadow. "We did it," he murmured, "all three of us."

Fifteen

The storm convinced Jay-jay that shelter was imperative. What if it ever snowed that hard? "Ready to commence building the space station," he said to Shadow, putting him in a hammock he'd made with the sleeping bag.

Jay-jay started working in the early morning and by noon had the planks set in place. He wrapped the head of the hammer in a piece of cloth so it would make less noise. About to drive a nail through the planks to the branch, Jay-jay missed and mashed his thumb.

He grimaced, sucking on his swelling finger. "And woodworking was the only class I was ever good in!" Then Jay-jay realized what he'd been about to do. Driving a nail into this tree would have been like hammering one into his own body.

"There's got to be some other way," Jay-jay said to Shadow, who alternately watched and napped. Jay-jay still had a good supply of rope left. Using a cross knot, he lashed the first plank to the limbs of the tree. He tested the wood, trying to twist it free, but it wouldn't budge. Satisfied, he went on. After he'd gotten the third plank securely tied in place Jay-jay had to stop. Ugly water blisters were puffing up on his palms. He bit through the skin and drained the fluid.

"What's needed here are some work gloves," he said to Shadow. Jay-jay snapped his fingers, took off his socks and poked five holes in the toes of each. Then he slipped them over his raw hands.

"Too bad I didn't think of it before I got the blisters," he said. "But I'll know for next time, and that's just as important."

It took the better part of the afternoon to get the floorboards lashed in place. Every so often, Jay-jay would slide down the rope to the ground to make sure the planking wasn't sticking out from the protective covering of leaves and branches.

Somehow, the burnished orange and gold leaves still clung to the tree. Jay-jay didn't know what he'd do when they finally fell. "Maybe by then, with the snow and the sleet it will be too cold for anybody to be wandering around here. What do you think, Shadow?"

Once during his labors, Jay-jay thought he heard somebody tramping through the bushes fringing the Great Hill. He listened intently. "It's just your imagination," he chided himself. "Or you would have growled, Shadow—right?"

At long last Jay-jay completed the foundation of the

castle. He stepped back and surveyed his work. The base measured some seven feet long by four feet wide. There were slight spaces between the floorboards where the rope kept the beams from butting together. It offended Jay-jay's sense of workmanship, and he wedged in strips of lathing.

There was still a gap here and there, but Jay-jay said, "That's okay, Shadow, because when it rains, we won't have any problems with drainage. Now for a roof over our heads."

About four feet above the platform a branch grew, extending way beyond the edge of the platform. Jay-jay flung the tarpaulin over the branch. He hammered nails all around the perimeter of the flooring, making sure never to drive the spikes into the living wood of the tree. Next, he attached foot-long lengths of rope to the grommet holes in the tarp.

Lashing these ropes to the spikes, the tent became as tight as a drum. Pitched, the tent occupied about one half of the floor space. When he struck the canvas and folded it back along the branch, it gave him nearly full use of the floor area.

While Jay-jay admired his construction, the leaves high above him suddenly rustled. Shadow looked up and managed a growl. Jay-jay saw bad-mouth squirrel fly through the air and land on a branch just above him.

The squirrel sat up, showing the white bib of his chest. Then he scratched his ear vigorously, darting suspicious glances at the new nuisance the intruder had built.

"Jealous, aren't you?" Jay-jay called to him.

The squirrel waggled his tail imperiously and let loose a tirade of shrill squeaks and pipings. Shadow barked and the squirrel scampered away.

Jay-jay shook his fist. "If I ever catch you—Shadow, what do you think of that rascal? Isn't it always the way? The minute you try to improve yourself, all the neighbors do is complain. Hey! You barked!" Jay-jay exclaimed. He scratched Shadow's head. "Good dog. You must be getting better."

For the last time that day Jay-jay slid down the ladder. He trudged wearily to the Loch and soaked his hot swollen hands.

With dusk, a stillness had fallen over the land. It was that magic hour just after the sun had set but still sent its pale memory over the curve of the earth. The wind that had quickened the day now barely ruffled the vegetation.

Though it was much too cold and made no sense, Jay-jay stripped off all his clothes. He stood naked, shivering in the blue air. He had never been naked outdoors before, and this baptismal try was weird and exciting at the same time.

Jay-jay waded into the Loch, the tingling water crept up his thighs and then to his bellybutton. Turning onto his back, Jay-jay felt the cool water supporting him, draining the aches of the day from his bones. Strange, he thought, it was warmer in the water than out.

So still and quiet did he float that after a bit a chickadee took a bath nearby, fluttering its wings against a reflected cloud. A chipmunk bounded into view, speckled brown against the sienna earth and its nose touched its water twin.

Jay-jay dogpaddled to the waterfall and stood under the Cascade, letting the torrents rush over his head and shoulders. He rubbed his body hard until all the weariness was washed away.

Bigger, he was definitely getting bigger. He could feel

it all over his body. And that stunted mood he'd always been in was somehow disappearing. Circling above him, Jay-jay spotted a red-winged hawk, and was amazed that he could see the bird without his glasses. Funny, he hadn't thought much about his specs since he'd broken them that first day.

Jay-jay raced out of the water, droplets glistening all over his skin. He rolled around on the grass to dry himself. There were angry rope burns where the lasso had dug into the flesh under his arms.

"But they'll go away soon enough," Jay-jay said, puffing out his chest. Though he was still mostly ribs, Jay-jay thought he detected a new muscle or two. "Soon I'll be able to take on anybody," he said, flexing a bicep. "Even somebody big as Elmo.

After he'd dressed, Jay-jay found an empty milk container and filled it with water. He brought it back to the oak and watered the ground. He made a dozen trips before he was satisfied that he'd replenished the tree and taken away any of the pain he might have caused it.

Later that night, with the castle solid beneath his feet and all right with his world, Jay-jay sat down to a celebration feast. First, he blew up the balloon Mrs. Miller had left tied to her bench, and set it afloat.

"As our banner," he told Shadow. "Don't worry. Nobody can see it in the dark. And in the morning we'll let the air out until tomorrow night."

Shadow sat up and poked his nose toward the food.

"Go ahead, you're invited," Jay-jay said. "Take your pick."

Shadow sniffed and made his selections very carefully.

There was a pizza pie crust with some tomato left on

it, though the cheese had turned to bubble gum. A pile of potato chips salvaged from six discarded bags. The carcass of the chicken, not quite picked to the bone. Their tankard of mead was the remains of a can of apple juice mixed with clear brook water. For dessert, Jay-jay had the last of the chocolate bar that still held the imprint of Mrs. Miller's terrified fingers.

Funny, Jay-jay thought, that seemed like it had happened a thousand years ago. But actually, only a few days had passed.

Jay-jay savored each mouthful of food. He'd never worked harder for a meal. He'd never eaten one that tasted better.

Suddenly Shadow's left ear stood up. The sound of footsteps crunching through leaves made the food stick in Jay-jay's throat. He flattened himself against the platform. Jay-jay put his hand over Shadow's muzzle to keep him from barking. Jay-jay peered over the edge. Too dark to make out anything. Gradually, the footsteps grew fainter and soon they were gone.

"Maybe it was just a guy and his girl looking for a place to make out?" Jay-jay whispered to Shadow. "No, that couldn't be, because I only heard one person. Well, whatever, I can't do anything about it now."

It took Jay-jay another half hour before he could relax. That was the second time today he'd heard somebody.

After dinner, Jay-jay put up the tent and stretched out beneath it, his head poking through the opening. Shadow lay next to him, breathing easier and occasionally teething on Jay-jay's finger.

Jay-jay looked up at the sky and the constellations

shining in their fierce patterns. He pointed through the skylight of leaves and traced the Big Dipper. How did that story go? A little match boy . . . and nobody would give him anything to eat. So when he died God flew him up to heaven and made him into the Big Dipper.

"Why couldn't He have just given him some food?" Jay-jay wondered sleepily. "And how come you've got to die first before He has any pity?" He sighed and said, "Shadow, you've got a star up there, Sirius, the Dog Star. That's what the guy at the Planetarium said. But I don't know which one it is."

Jay-jay gave a great big yawn. "Wish I knew what was going on up there. But I don't." And so he contented himself with it being a mystery beyond his knowing. "Someday, maybe," he murmured, "when I'm an astronaut and I can fly anyplace I want."

The slow swing of the stars seemed to ebb and flow in his sight. His eyelids fluttered as he drifted to a secret place that was half sleep, half reverie. He felt his body grow hard, felt his limbs pulse and then he started to float. An inch at first, then two. Then off the platform and up through the branches without holding on!

I'm going to do it, I'm doing it! Jay-jay realized with an awesome sense of terror and amazement.

He was about to clear the tree and be fully airborne when he woke with violent stomach cramps. The food he'd eaten must have been contaminated.

Jay-jay made it down to the ground and then threw up. After the weakness had passed, he managed to climb back up to the castle where an anxious Shadow waited.

A seed of injustice sprouted in Jay-jay, a seed that mushroomed until it pushed every other thought from his mind.

Was it fitting and just that the Prince of Central Park—and his retinue—be forced to live on scraps and leavings? Was it fitting and just that his dreams be ruined?

"No it's not!" Jay-jay cried, bolting upright and spooking Shadow.

Just as he had liberated wood and tools to build his home, so he must liberate food for his body. That was the secret to his survival.

"Food should be free anyway, Shadow. Why shouldn't people have all they need to eat? Think of how those frankfurter rolls would have tasted with a frankfurter in them?"

Shadow wagged his tail.

Jay-jay's mouth watered at the thought of all the Sabrett stands in the park, with the aroma of meat and vegetables coming from the Zoo Cafeteria.

"No!" he exclaimed, punching his palm. "No stands and no cafeteria!"

Shadow gave a complaining sigh and turned the other way.

"Tomorrow I will demand tribute from a place worthy of my rank and station."

Tomorrow, Jay-jay thought, drifting off to dreams of milk and cookies, tomorrow the Prince of Central Park would demand tribute from the richest inn in his realm, the Tavern on the Green.

Sixteen

"You're who?" the aging porter in the spattered white uniform asked, cupping his ear at Jay-jay.

Jay-jay shifted from leg to leg in the cavernous kitchen of the Tavern on the Green. He'd never have guessed it was so big, bigger than his school gymnasium.

Minutes before, Jay-jay had hiked himself up on the outside loading platform where the trucks were making their weekend deliveries. Sides of beef, cartloads of bread, cases of milk and vegetables. The staples would be twisted and baked and manipulated into delicacies for the fortunate few.

Nobody had paid any attention to Jay-jay, and he had followed his nose down the dingy corridors to the kitchen. The bustle of chefs and porters, the hum of dishwashers, and waiters rushing about balancing trays of food made Jay-jay's head spin. And the smells! Shrimp in deep fryers, bacon sizzling on the cast-iron stoves, everything made his mouth water.

Days too long to count had passed since he'd had a decent meal; with Mrs. Miller gone, Jay-jay couldn't rely on her daily treat.

Jay-jay pulled his eyes away from the food, grabbed the porter's sleeve and repeated his rank and station. It was so simple! They had so much, how could they refuse him?

"What are you crazy or something?" the old busboy demanded, hands akimbo. "I work here and I have to pay for my own food. Think we have eats to throw away on every kid who shows up?"

Jay-jay started to argue, but the porter feinted at him. "Beat it, before I give you a swift kick in the ass."

Dodging the foot, Jay-jay backed out. All the while his brain was photographing the layout, refrigerators, skylights, exits.

Outside in the sunlit Saturday afternoon, Jay-jay squared his shoulders, skirted the formal garden, trudged past the window walls of the dining room where the forks and spoons never stopped, and went to the front entrance.

Jay-jay muttered, "You should have known better than to deal with hirelings. That skullery lout is too dumb to recognize royalty. Go right to the top."

Under the green and yellow canopy he marched, past the large yellow sign that read: "We Are Closed on Mondays."

A patent-leather man who smelled very clean looked down at Jay-jay. He began to negotiate. The man barked with laughter. Remembering the proverb he'd learned in English, "A soft voice turneth away wrath, a harsh voice incurreth anger," Jay-jay explained with all the sweet reasonableness he could muster.

Jay-jay heard his voice getting higher, heard his demands echo through the jammed banquet rooms where a political fund-raising party was going on. . . . "Shadow to take care of . . . tribute. . . ."

A manicured hand descended on Jay-jay's collar, another grabbed the seat of his pants, and he was hustled unceremoniously through the door.

Jay-jay picked himself up from the grass and shook his fist at the brick walls and the clusters of towers disguised to look like chimneys. "Okay," he shouted. "I gave you your chance. Now it's no quarter!"

The heck with that proverb, he thought, as he snagged a bag of trash from the garbage cans before the busboy chased him away. Nothing he could eat, but Jay-jay pocketed a couple of wine corks and a half-used can of Sterno.

Climbing a small hill just north of the Tavern, Jay-jay looked down at the seemingly impregnable structure. "Closed on Mondays, huh?" he repeated. Good. This being Saturday, it gave him plenty of time to work out a campaign. He scratched numbers in the hard-packed earth. "Twenty-four and twelve, let's see, roughly thirty-six hours. Hell! If I can't figure out how to breach their defenses in that time, then I don't deserve to rule."

Remembering how much the Cedar Hill construction map had helped him, Jay-jay drew as detailed a plan of the inn as he could. Lots of things he just guessed at, and lots of other things, like passageways that ran between the angled buildings, were dictated by common sense.

"Sunday night, after closing," Jay-jay said. "That's when I'll strike. Check for watchmen first. Find the terminals for the burglar alarm system.

"Maybe there aren't any?" he said hopefully.

Nah, there always were, like in *Mission Impossible*, and *It Takes a Thief* and the rest of the good-guy robbery flicks.

Then Jay-jay had a thought. Instead of looting the place totally, why not take only the amount he and Shadow could eat in say, a week? "Otherwise, everything will turn rotten," he told himself. "This way, the restaurant will keep my food fresh. Then every Sunday I raid the Tavern and replenish my supply."

When it got really cold, then he'd make off with the big haul because he'd be able to store everything outside. "For the first time in your life, go to the head of the class," Jay-jay said, hitching his thumbs under his armpits.

Could he get past the guards? Outwit the deadly laser beam electric eye? Crack all the combinations and open the refrigerators? And without disturbing anything so they'll never know the Prince had struck!

"You'd just better!" Jay-jay exclaimed, and his stomach seconded that loudly.

Heading uptown, Jay-jay cut away from the macadam footpath and followed the bridle path. He liked the rich smell of the occasional droppings of manure and the feel of the springy loam underfoot.

Out of a cloud of dust and a thunder of hooves came the mighty—only some roly-poly dude dressed in fancy jodhpurs trying to rein a wheeling, snorting, pawing palomino.

Will I ever command such a majestic mount? Jay-jay wondered. "It would make patrolling my territory so much easier." Instead of trudging to trouble spots he'd come galloping up! Put down invasions from marauding vandals.

"To say nothing of muggers," Jay-jay cried with a sword slash through the air. The medallion bounced around his neck and Jay-jay tucked it into his shirt. Then, with the recollection of Elmo's crazed eyes burning into his, Jay-jay's hand moved to massage his throat.

"He *couldn't* have recognized me! It all happened too fast!"

Jay-jay knew that Elmo would burn him, finish him off without a second thought, if he ever caught him. "I just hope that the cops threw the key away!"

Approaching the Woman's Gate at Seventy-second Street, Jay-jay's step dragged. He passed under an arbor of tangled vines where two bees zigzagged among tiny, hardy flowers.

"If only I could eat flowers," Jay-jay said, watching them. When a bee ate a flower it came out honey. But when a human being ate anything . . . it made Jay-jay wonder just who the advanced creatures really were.

Once he crossed Seventy-second, the terrain grew wooded with empress trees, staghorn sumac and bursts of magnolia. Down seven stone steps and seven again into a shaded glen that dipped and curved. A cathedral arch of oak and walnut spread their boughs above and light filtered through the stained glass leaves. One leaf fell, hesitated, fell, and skittered across his path.

Jay-jay scooped it up and held it in his palm. Slowly,

he closed his fingers and crushed autumn into winter. A cold wind seemed to moan through him. Winter . . . what will I do when the snows fall? When I'll leave tracks wherever I go? When food . . . All at once it got too much for Jay-jay and he sank to his knees against a gigantic erratic left by the Ice Age thousands of years before. The boulder was black and barren.

"Like everything about trying to make it here," Jay-jay whispered. Give it up, a weary voice whimpered. Go back to them. Lead their kind of life, they've won.

Jay-jay struggled to his knees. His gaze traveled to the top of the great tombstone. On the crest of the solid mountain, right out of the rock! Grew a sapling.

A shot of adrenalin coursed through Jay-jay. Picking his way carefully, he climbed to the young spindle tree. He inspected the base of the reedy trunk. Solid stone, no soil anywhere. Yet somehow the sapling was drawing nourishment through whatever crevices there were in the rock.

Jay-jay marveled at the tree's will. For it had struck roots down through twenty feet of stone. Impossible, for a tiny seed to survive such odds. But the branches that spread out above him were testimony not only of survival but of growth.

Jay-jay slid down the huge gravestone, bumping along on his bony behind. His step became lighthearted, almost jaunty again.

"You can make it," he said fiercely. "You will make it. Just go deep. That's the answer. Deep."

The heavy foliage thinned; to the right of the path, the Lake came into view. Jay-jay scooted across the West Drive and circled the expanse of water.

A band of men jogged toward him looking lumpy in their gray sweat clothes. A spit of land protruded into the lake and Jay-jay ventured onto Hernshead Peninsula. He followed the rocky promontory to its end and watched the few rowboats that dotted the lake.

The view to the north and east was of the Ramble. Jay-jay had explored it once. Thicker than a jungle it was, and a lot of heavy sex went on in those bushes during the weekend. Best to stay away.

To the south, above the park's autumn colors and the sulphurous haze of an inversion, were the towers of the city, ominous stalagmites dripped from a poisoned sky.

Jay-jay sat down and hugged his knees. Slowly, he became aware that his park was surrounded on all sides by these menacing stone towers. They reminded him of something. All at once he remembered the dinosaur's jaws and it seemed to him those jaws were like the maw of this carnivorous city, whose spires were jagged teeth, ever ready to devour him and his park.

Nearby, a couple of people were fishing and Jay-jay decided to try his luck. He emptied his pockets and came up with a length of string, the wine cork and a safety pin. Next, he overturned a clod of earth and baited the pin with a worm. He cast the line and waited expectantly.

Minutes passed. Jay-jay fidgeted and squirmed. "City fish get pretty smart. Maybe you'd better disguise the line?" He spotted a cluster of witch hazel flowers, the last of the season, and plucked one. Very carefully, he wound the stem around the cork and cast it in a slow, cautious swing lest the flower fall off.

"Come on," Jay-jay prayed to the gods of wind and water, *"please.* I've got a sick dog at home."

Two monarch butterflies fluttered into sight. They hovered above the mirror of the lake and then one landed on top of the cork, its wings folding and unfolding. The other flitted around the bobbing yellow flower, trying to land also. A sunfish torpedoed up from the depths and struck the bait just as the butterfly darted off.

With a yowl, Jay-jay hauled in his catch. Repeating what he'd seen the other fishermen do, Jay-jay scaled and filleted the fish with his pocketknife. He lit the Sterno, speared the fillets deftly with a twig and broiled them over the smoky blue flame.

When the fillets were sizzling brown, Jay-jay wrapped Shadow's portion in a piece of discarded wax paper and then ate his piece. With every mouthful a glow began to radiate from his stomach. It was the first hot food he'd had since he'd jumped into the pool at the Met. When he was done, Jay-jay picked his teeth delicately with the stalk of a cattail.

The feast had made Jay-jay logy. "Shadow can wait a minute or two," he said, sprawling out on the ground. The waters of the lake shimmered, the trees and sky quivered and broke into unrecognizable pieces as the Loch Monster, disguised as a line of ducklings paddled by.

The broken pieces slowly fit themselves together and then a face appeared in the stilled waters. Before Jay-jay could collect his wits, a rowboat rammed onto the shore and a guy hopped out.

"Gotcha!" cried Elmo.

Part Four

Seventeen

"Let me go! What are you, crazy or something?" Jay-jay yelled, trying the big lie. "What do you want? Let me go!"

But Elmo had already fastened on the medallion around Jay-jay's neck. His sharp glance took in the surroundings. Too many people around. He grabbed Jay-jay's arm and twisted it behind his back.

"What do I want?" Elmo spat, shoving Jay-jay toward the boat. "Wait until we get out in the middle of the lake, then you'll see what I want."

Jay-jay kicked and squirmed, trying to break Elmo's hold. When he tried to yell for help, Elmo clamped his hand over his mouth. Then Elmo picked Jay-jay up and dumped him in the rowboat. Elmo jumped in and tried to cast off, but with Jay-jay's extra weight, the boat stayed beached. Elmo cursed, hopped out again, put his shoulder to the prow and shoved.

As Elmo heaved, Jay-jay saw his chance. He grabbed an oar and poled the boat away before Elmo could get back in. Elmo shouted and leaped into the water after him. Clutching both oars, Jay-jay rowed with all his might. Elmo came within an arm's length of the stern, hands grasping, but he was knee-deep now and the mucky bottom slowed him. Jay-jay managed to spin the boat out into deep water.

Elmo looked around wildly. He couldn't swim after the little son-of-a-bitch, the water was too cold. Head him off on land, that's what he'd have to do.

Oars grinding in the oarlocks, Jay-jay pulled toward the center of the lake. "But I can't stay stuck here in the middle forever," he panted.

Time was on Elmo's side. Sooner or later, Jay-jay would have to land. The boathouse, Jay-jay decided. There'd be a guard on duty; that would stop Elmo. Jay-jay headed south and then east toward the Bow Bridge. Through the gentle arch of the bridge he could see the wooden docks and the quaint structure of the boathouse.

Elmo guessed Jay-jay's destination. To get to the boathouse from Hernshead Peninsula, Elmo had to make a wide circuit. He sprinted along the rocky path that followed the shoreline, taking the turn around Cherry Hill at the lake's southernmost point.

"You've got to row like you've never rowed before," Jay-jay said through gritted teeth, then realized that he'd never done *any* rowing.

The lake narrowed at Bow Bridge. "Narrow enough," Elmo breathed, "so if I reach it first. . . ." He'd be waiting at the bridge railing and when Jay-jay passed beneath him, Elmo would drop into the boat.

Jay-jay tracked Elmo as he crashed through the thickets. When Jay-jay saw the bridge coming up, he knew that Elmo was going to head him off. Too late to turn back. Jay-jay felt his arms tearing out of their sockets as he pulled harder.

"I'm not going to make it!" Jay-jay gasped, seeing Elmo closing the gap. They would reach the bridge at almost the same time. Goose pimples swept over Jay-jay. Maybe he'll just beat up on me and then leave me be? he thought hopefully. But he knew that was wishful thinking. The look in Elmo's eyes meant more than just a beating.

When it seemed all was lost, the wind shifted and blew in strong from the west, setting up a favorable current. It was enough to urge the boat through the bow of the underpass just as Elmo raced overhead onto the bridge.

Elmo swung his legs over the railing—a second too late! The boat skimmed away from him.

"You little bastard!" Elmo shouted. "You're not getting the best of me! No way!"

Jay-jay watched Elmo race off the bridge and swing toward Bethesda Fountain. Elmo made better time now, the path no longer meandered but led straight to the boathouse. Jay-jay searched vainly for somebody at the dock. Guard is probably goofing off, he thought, scared out of his skin. He looked around desperately for anybody else who might intervene, but even the twin stone steps on either side of the fountain were empty of people.

Start yelling! Jay-jay thought in a panic. But who would hear him?

Holding the right oar steady, Jay-jay paddled furiously with the left until the prow came about and he was turned toward the shoreline of the Ramble.

Elmo sprinted onto the boathouse dock, and kicked the piling when he saw Jay-jay making for the opposite shore. Then he realized the ramifications and said, "That's it. The Ramble is even better." When he cornered the little punk in there, there'd be nobody to stop him.

"I won't lose you this time," Elmo muttered. The kid's blue windbreaker with the sunburst stood out like a bull's-eye

Elmo started around the north shore of the lake. "I *can't* lose him this time," Elmo said in cadence with his stride. With his trial coming up, Elmo couldn't take the chance that Jay-jay might come out of the park and testify against him.

Jay-jay's brain worked feverishly. No good just trying to get home to the castle. Because with Elmo so close on his heels, the maniac would know exactly where he lived. "The only way is to shake him, somehow."

The Ramble was coming up fast. Even as the boat ground onto the shore Jay-jay was out and running for the dense forest.

Up the steep hill Jay-jay scrambled, paying no heed to the branches lashing his face and the thorns tearing at his clothes. What do I have, three, maybe four minute head start? Where's the best place to hide? In the brush? Or someplace where there's a lot of people—the Zoo! But that lay south, and Elmo had cut him off from that direction.

North was the best way. The Twenty-second Police Precinct at Eighty-fifth Street, that would cool Elmo.

But then the cops would grab him too, ask questions. No, the cops and Elmo both meant the same thing, the end of his new life.

Jay-jay's feet were flying faster than his thoughts. Hurdling the dry riverbed of the Gill, darting along the winding paths, startling some people who were thrashing about in the bushes, running and running until he finally broke into a clearing. The red brick building of the Fire Alarm Station lay directly ahead.

He had to choose now. Either across the Seventy-ninth Street Transverse at Belvedere Castle, or—he struck out east, to the rise of Cedar Hill where the red dinosaur still dominated the construction site.

At the ridge, Jay-jay fell to his knees, sucking in air. He *had* to rest! He searched the area; Elmo was nowhere in sight. "That doesn't mean anything," Jay-jay warned himself. He hadn't seen Elmo until he'd risen from the lake like some avenging demon.

The east overpass of the Seventy-ninth Street Transverse gained, Jay-jay once again scanned the terrain. Damn! There he was! At the far end of the Cedar Hill parking lot. Elmo was running first one way then the other, as though trying to sniff out Jay-jay's trail.

Jay-jay dropped to the grass. He didn't think Elmo had spotted him, but with that slippery one you couldn't be sure of anything. Keeping as low a profile as he could, Jay-jay scurried toward the crowds of people at the Metropolitan Museum.

Red and yellow buses were unloading schoolchildren for a Saturday outing at the Met. About two hundred kids streamed onto the sidewalk, milling about, their sharp cries cutting the air. They arranged themselves into classes, some thirty in each. An instructor was in charge of each group.

With the ingenuity of the hunted, Jay-jay joined the group of kids who were about his size, quickly losing himself in the crowd now surging toward the museum's entrance.

They're rich kids from some private school, Jay-jay decided. Because they all had braces on their teeth.

From the top of the entrance staircase, Jay-jay's eyes swept over the approaches to the building. Nothing from the north. Nothing in front of him. Then he saw Elmo round the south corner of the building. Jay-jay pressed toward the revolving doors and they swept him into the museum.

Eighteen

In the awesome vault of the Great Hall, a momentary hush fell over the throng of children. Then their irrepressible voices babbled up again.

Swept across the shiny terrazzo floor, Jay-jay tried to convince himself that in all these dozens of rooms Elmo would never find him.

All you've got to do is keep out of sight for another hour, he assured himself. By then it will be dark and you'll lose him easy.

"Now, class, I want you to pay attention," the teacher said to the students clustered around her. "Remember we studied this in—"

"Yes, Mrs. Munjack." "Are we going to get a test on this, Mrs. Munjack?" "Which way are the mummies, Mrs. Munjack?"

Into the Egyptian Section they swarmed, to circle before the Mastaba of Peri-Nebi.

"Who was he?" a chubby student asked, nudging Jay-jay.

Jay-jay hunched his shoulders.

"Say, you're not in our class," the plump boy said, looking at Jay-jay over the rim of his sunglasses. But when he saw Jay-jay's stricken look he added, "That's okay. You can tag along with us. My name's Alan, but everybody calls me Chubby."

"Hi, Alan," Jay-jay said.

The students' voices, high and querulous with each new find, began to get to Jay-jay. From the past he remembered when he'd lent his own voice to such a din. He held back his urge to join in but heard, "Look at that mummy! Gee, was that a person?" coming from a throat that somehow did not seem like his.

Jay-jay flushed with happiness. It felt good to be a kid again. To forget about having to rip off the Tavern on the Green. Forget about some nut who was chasing him. Just be carefree and—but a glimpse of Elmo coming down a long corridor shocked Jay-jay back to reality.

Elmo had popped up too close to the main entrance for Jay-jay to sneak out without being seen. "Best to stay hidden with all these kids," he said.

"What?" Chubby asked. Then his nose wrinkled. "I smell fish."

A harassed Mrs. Munjack counted off ten students at a time and sent them through the tunnel-like entrance into the crypt. Waiting his turn, Jay-jay stole a look at Mrs. Munjack. She was pretty, dressed real mod. Her big round glasses gave her a startled look. Matter of fact, he noticed, all the teachers were wearing glasses.

Guess you can't be a teacher without specs, Jay-jay reasoned, the way you can't be a construction worker without a hard hat. It must come from living in cubicles, hemmed in by walls until your eyeballs got lazy and finally atrophied.

"Well," Jay-jay said, "that will never happen to the Prince of Central Park."

"Who?" Chubby asked. His pants had a tendency to creep up his behind and as he yanked at them his clipboard tipped and his papers spilled across the floor. Chubby whimpered as he squatted to pick them up.

Instead of giving him a hand, his classmates jeered and kicked at the notes as their group filed into the tomb.

I'm a dumb ass to help him, Jay-jay thought; he'd never do it for me. But, remembering the not-so-long-ago when he'd been the scapegoat, Jay-jay knelt anyway. Between them, they had the papers collected in seconds, and Jay-jay had made a friend for life.

The narrow opening of the burial chamber seemed to close in on Jay-jay. The students' hushed voices sounded hollow in the mummy's tomb. Clusters of people marched sideways along the walls. Jay-jay tried to figure out what the people in the five-thousand-year-old drawings were doing. Pretty much the same thing everybody was doing today. Living, eating, sleeping, screwing.

"What will it be like five thousand years from now?" Jay-jay wondered aloud.

"We'll never last that long?" Chubby said.

Jay-jay said under his breath, "Some of us will."

The next bunch of students pushed their way into the entrance of the narrow tomb, forcing Jay-jay's group out the exit.

A wide-eyed blond girl who looked distressed tugged at the teacher's hand. "What happens to you when you're dead like that, Mrs. Munjack?"

Mrs. Munjack stroked the girl's hair. "Why, nobody knows. It's one of the great mysteries."

"I know," Jay-jay whispered to Chubby. "You're reborn. Know what else?"

"What?"

"You don't have to die to do it."

Chubby stared at him. "Who says? You? Then, smart aleck, who don't you raise your hand and tell that to Mrs. Munjack?"

But Jay-jay kept his mouth shut, sorry that he'd called so much attention to himself. Already Mrs. Munjack had given him a puzzled look or two.

They moved on to the French Impressionist painters on the second floor. Jay-jay blinked at the flowers that sparkled with sunlight. Then they went into the Baroque section where the whole world looked like one big baloney curl.

Then the American Wing . . . Twentieth-Century Art . . . the minutes ticked away bringing dusk and safety closer to Jay-jay.

"Bet your teacher doesn't take take you into the Indian Art gallery," Jay-jay said to Chubby.

"Why not?" Chubby asked.

"Because they've got *some* statue in there! Of a man and a woman," Jay-jay said knowingly. *"The Amorous Couple."*

"No kidding?" Chubby said, intrigued. "How do you know?"

Jay-jay shrugged nonchalantly. "Oh, I come here a·

lot. Know something else? There's exactly twenty-three steps down to the first landing of the Great Staircase, and twenty-three more down to the main floor.''

Chubby counted as the class started down the steps. When they reached the lobby he gazed at Jay-jay with a look approaching adoration.

"I've been here before!" Jay-jay said with a thrill of recognition as the class made their way into the gloom of the Medieval Hall. Jay-jay stopped at a reconstructed altar and stared up at a wooden crucifix. Painted blood dripped from the spear wounds and three spikes held the man in a triangle of death. Jay-jay caught himself rubbing his palms. He tore his eyes away from the cross and locked eyes with Elmo.

Elmo's lips parted, revealing his discolored teeth. His eyes flicked to Jay-jay's jacket.

How could I have been so dumb! Jay-jay thought, in that instant realizing that his sunburst windbreaker had given him away.

Keeping a wary eye on Mrs. Munjack, who was too busy counting noses to notice anything, Elmo skillfully edged through the group of kids toward Jay-jay, as though separating a calf about to be branded. Elmo's wet shoes were a constant reminder to him of how the little bastard had humiliated him at the lake. And when he recalled mugging the old lady, Elmo's head pounded so he thought he was having a convulsion.

Get a grip on yourself, Elmo commanded. You'll have your hands on him in a minute. His trembling fingers closed around the switchblade in his pocket. One jab, that's all it would take. Then in all the confusion, he'd disappear into the crowd. Elmo's heart thudded as he worked his way closer. For the chase had given Elmo a thrill he'd never known before. He had the taste of blood in his mouth . . . and it tasted good. . . .

As the class headed for the French Rooms, Jay-jay made his move. Bolting from the group, he dashed down a long corridor lined with heavy wooden furniture. Elmo ran after, slowing only when he startled two matrons sitting on a bench.

The chase led them through the great sounding halls of the medieval exhibits, past the mounted knights and heraldic banners. Past the tapestry where the unicorn still fled and bled. Past all the works that had been touched by the creator, ran Jay-jay, with Elmo gaining.

A domed window at the end of a hallway let in the failing daylight. If I can find an exit and make it out into the park, Jay-jay thought desperately, as his numbed legs carried him around the exhibit cases. Elmo was too strong, too fast! Got to stop to breathe!

"If I don't think of something fast I'm a goner," Jay-jay gasped as he stumbled into another room. "I'm running in circles!" Just ahead of him was Mrs. Munjack and her class. They were lined up at the rest rooms, filing in by sixes prior to their bus trip home.

Jay-jay fell into the boy's line, quickly insinuating himself next to Chubby, who was close to the bathroom door.

Elmo charged up just as Jay-jay's group went inside. Elmo spotted Mrs. Munjack. Don't try anything with her so close, he warned himself. Wait down the corridor. Till the kids leave.

In the tiled bathroom, Jay-jay grabbed Chubby's arm. He choked for breath. "There's a crazy guy out there trying to get me," he blurted. "What am I going to do?"

Chubby dropped his clipboard again. "Tell Mrs. Munjack? No? Hide? No? Disguise yourself?" he stammered.

Jay-jay sprang into action. He whipped off his jacket, reversed it to the plain blue side and put it back on. Then he went to the sink and after taking great gulps of water, he wet his hair, plastering it down flat against his head. Chubby snatched off his sunglasses and handed them to Jay-jay.

Jay-jay stared at the reflection in the mirror and a totally different boy looked back. "Now here's what you've got to do," he said urgently to Chubby. "You've got to walk out with me."

Chubby shrank back. "I can't! I'm scared! I didn't pee yet!"

"Please!" Jay-jay begged. He threw his arm around Chubby's shoulder. "Keep talking to me."

"About what?"

"It doesn't matter. Just keep talking until we get to the end of the corridor."

Arms around each other's shoulders, they walked out of the bathroom. Chubby kept up a banter about how great the museum was and football and how next week in science class they were going to mate hamsters and how he'd sure like to see that statue, talking a mile a minute as they marched past Elmo, who had his eyes glued to the Men's Room door, waiting for the sunburst jacket to appear.

Jay-jay and Chubby sauntered toward the end of the corridor. Without losing step, Jay-jay took off the sunglasses and handed them back.

Chubby said in a rush, "Sometimes my mother lets me travel on weekends, maybe we could—?"

"Sure," Jay-jay said. "I'll be in the park whenever you come."

Jay-jay continued walking, keeping his step measured, knowing that if he panicked and ran, Elmo would be after him like a shot.

As he turned the corner of the corridor, Jay-jay made a dash for it, turning once for a final wave to Chubby. He fled across the marble lobby and out into the deep dusk to disappear into the safety of his wild realm.

Jay-jay was well past the obelisk when he heard the distant shouts. He stopped, barely able to make out the cries.

"I'll get you! Count on it! You'll see! I'll—"

"And I'm tired of running," Jay-jay whispered. "I'll be ready for you."

Nineteen

"So that's why I'm late, Shadow,"
Jay-jay explained.

Shadow gave him a baleful look, turned away and
rested his head on his paws.

"You've got every right to be sore, but did you have to
do it right in the middle of the living room?" Jay-jay
grumbled, cleaning up the signs of Shadow's annoyance.
"Well, if you're that spiteful, I guess you're all better."

Jay-jay unwrapped the aluminum foil and laid the
fillets in front of Shadow's nose. "Here's your dinner.
Cooked it myself. There's nothing better than cold
sunfish."

Shadow resisted about a second longer and then
decided to forgive Jay-jay.

* * *

Jay-jay went to bed early, exhausted by the day. He watched a bright star appear on the horizon. Was that Venus? he wondered. Then a red-tinted one. That must be Mars. Soon a million stars whirled on his eyelids.

Then as he drifted into deeper sleep, Jay-jay became aware that something was stalking him. Unknown, relentless. The only escape was up, airborne or die.

Like a sleepwalker, Jay-jay moved to the brink of the platform, arms raised to the saving wind. But it did not come. Somewhere from the center of his being a voice called, "One thing only holds you down. Fear keeps you trapped in your own shadow. Try!"

"But there's no wind!" Jay-jay yelled back.

"The wish shall be your carrier. Some drive their chin into the north star. Surrender, and you shall soar without moving and capture green wind."

And so Jay-jay stretched, wider, while the deadly presence crept closer. Trying beyond all endurance, an intoxication came over him and slowly, very slowly, Jay-jay felt himself rise off the platform. An inch . . . and then he was floating up through the branches . . . about to leave the protection of the oak. He cried out in panic, steeling himself for the fall, but instead he saw his ground-shadow dwindling to a speck.

Seized then with the glory of flight, he soared into a sky without limit, dove into bottomless seas, spun upward again to a weightless world where he breathed an atmosphere of ecstasy.

Below, the earth turned like a giant brain, patterned, controlled, while he rose to the endless void. Borne on spirit and grace, he ascended, past clusters of rushing flowers that turned into stars, onward toward a secret spawning of the galaxies where he burned with such intensity he was transformed into the heart of a star, racing toward the moment of supreme unity, exploding into a stunned, awake and transformed Jay-jay.

Sunday's child woke to the resounding carillon of "Sheep May Safely Graze" from St. John's the Divine. All about him leaves moved and murmured, dappling his castle with gold and orange and russet light.

A flock of geese arrowed their way across a sky of such serene clarity that the trees seemed to be crying leaves of joy. Jay-jay came down from his tree only once, in the early morning. For even in this remote region, dazed people wandered about, eager to capture autumn's penultimate moment. To walk was to crush brightness.

All through the day Jay-jay stayed quiet, wondering over his dream and his newfound powers. The night's upcoming events demanded that he conserve his strength and so he did no further experimenting but contented himself with the marvel of his being that had allowed him to experience the stars.

Jay-jay tried to say a prayer. After all, it was Sunday. "With what's ahead of me, I'll need all the help I can get."

Shadow's tail thumped and Jay-jay said, "Sorry, you can't come. You'd only get in the way. And make sure you don't—" He shook his finger.

Though the run-in with Elmo had shaken him severely, Jay-jay knew he had no other choice but to go ahead with the Tavern heist. Stocking a supply of food was the only way he and Shadow would survive the winter. This night would decide if he would live or die in his park.

"The Lord is my shepherd . . ." Jay-jay began, "and

to the Republic, for which it stands . . . nuts." He shrugged helplessly.

He couldn't remember anything, not a proverb, motto, or a psalm. "Not even the Lord's Prayer, and I used to know that one by heart," he told Shadow, feeling a twinge of uneasiness. How fast he was forgetting the things of the stone world.

Yet there was so much that was worthwhile, so much that he didn't want to forget. "As soon as everything is set," he said to Shadow, "then I'll go back to the Museum of Natural History, and the Planetarium, the Metropolitan and the Arsenal. See, Shadow, all those places have books—" Money, Jay-jay thought suddenly. Books cost. Well, he'd get it somehow, the way he'd managed everything else. And he would teach himself the things he wanted to learn.

Wouldn't it be great to know all the constellations? For his next visit! To know the kinds of rocks in the park and how old they were? Or if there were any edible roots or plants around, the way Caine on *Kung Fu* always found them.

As the day drifted by, Jay-jay alternately jotted down things he planned to study and listed his blessings. He felt the solidness of the platform beneath him, touched the tough canvas tent. He felt so grateful for all he and Shadow had that he wanted to acknowledge it someway, anyway.

Absently, he picked up a fallen golden leaf and held it to the sinking sun. The light shone through, revealing the translucent veins.

"Then I will say a prayer to you," Jay-jay said, gripping a branch of the oak. "So that you will grow again. And a prayer to the colors in the sky. One to the squirrel. And to the old lady, Mrs. Miller. A prayer to whoever threw away that sleeping bag. To my father. To my mother. To Alan-Chubby who saved me. To Shadow! To me! To Elmo. Yes, even to Elmo.''

And so, from the simple seared leaf lying in his palm, Jay-jay's prayer reached out to embrace everything, great and small.

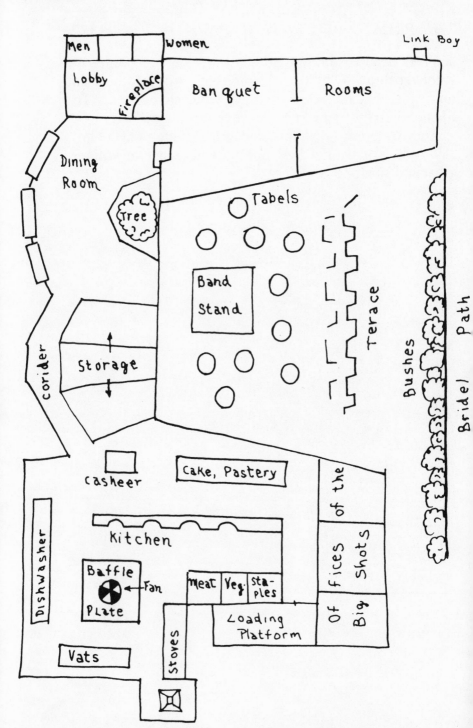

Tavern on the Green

Twenty

Night came like a thief. A distant church bell tolled eleven. Jay-jay lit the sterno and in its flickering light carefully memorized the floor plan he had drawn of the Tavern on the Green.

"And make sure you figure a way to get *out* this time," Jay-jay said, remembering his dilemma at the construction camp.

He packed his canvas knapsack with the screwdriver and matches and the Sterno and slung it over his shoulder. Jay-jay hugged Shadow good-bye. Then, with darkness as a shroud, he set out.

From the rise of the Adventure Playground, the Tavern complex spread before him. Wide bands of light shone from the picture windows picking out the dark masses of surrounding shrubs and trees.

Keeping to the shadows, Jay-jay approached stealthily. The hubbub of music and laughter grew louder. He made a wide circle around the building and ducked into the boxwood hedge at the edge of the flagstone terrace.

Most of the party was going on inside of the banquet hall, but some fair maidens in long gowns and handsome men in tuxedos danced outside under a fantasy of swaying lanterns. And infrared heaters. Just above the bandstand was a large electric clock whose hands stood at midnight. To the right, a sign read:

Occupancy by More Than 1092 People
Is Unlawful and Dangerous.

Jay-jay let out a long silent whistle. A lot of people meant a lot of food.

A police car cruised by, making its slow rounds around the Taven. Jay-jay burrowed deeper into the bushes and made a mental note of the time. He could have reached out and touched the car fender as it passed by, and he wondered if it was the same two cops who had almost cornered him at the Reservoir. When the prowl car disappeared, Jay-jay turned his attention to the party.

Waiters rushed about, balancing trays groaning with food. A single tray would keep me and Shadow going for a week, Jay-jay thought. A woman whose bazooms were so big they looked like one huge one was laughing fit to bust at one table. At another, a man was guzzling champagne right out of the bottle.

Jay-jay squirmed against the hard ground. His mouth had gone dry at the sight of all the food almost within arm's reach. Yet so far away, it might have been on another planet.

He was on the outside, looking in. He had always been on the outside. Lying there, his fingers clutching tufts of grass, Jay-jay made a startling discovery.

"I'll *always* be on the outside looking in!"

A rage began to build in him. Against *them*. It made him want to smash their bottles of liquor, overturn their tables. Punch their faces.

At twelve thirty, the police car made another appearance. "Half-hour intervals," Jay-jay whispered, checking the clock. "If only I can depend on that."

A polka, a lot of rock and roll that Jay-jay recognized, a cha-cha, a waltz, then a slow fox trot as the music wound down. The band dragged on to "Goodnight Ladies." Everybody kissed each other and swore they'd never had such a good time and one gent was throwing up in the bushes to prove it, and limousines rolled to the entrance and a princess rode off in a magenta hansom drawn by a white horse and now the relieved waiters were bustling about, cleaning up the wreckage.

At one o'clock, the prowl car again. And again at one thirty when the last of the lanterns twinkled off, and the manager locked the doors, leaving the building dark and empty.

Jay-jay forced himself to wait five minutes; people were always forgetting things and coming back. He crept from the bushes and circled the U-shaped building. First he tried all the doors; no outside doorknobs on any of them so the locks couldn't be picked the way he'd done the grammar school health office.

His next impulse was to break one of the French windows, get in fast, pillage the kitchen, and get out. But

a little voice warned him that breaking a window was a
trap. At the building's rear wing, Jay-jay came across a
small red box placed almost out of sight in a window.
"Link-Boy" read the label on the alarm box.
"Probably means it's linked up with every door and
window in the place." Break or enter any one of them
without the right keys and the burglar alarm would go
off.
"At least you're listening to yourself now," Jay-jay
said. "Good thing you learned that much."
The whole building was beginning to smell like one
great big cake. But how to get in? "There's got to be a
way," he said. "Remember how tough you thought
Cedar Hill would be?" A sudden thought crossed his
mind. This will be my third break-in! Jeez! Is the world
making a crook out of me?
On the south side of the restaurant, Jay-jay spotted a
vent set in the brick wall. It was the duct for the air
conditioner. He measured the opening against his body.
Nope, not big enough to crawl through.
Hugging the wall, Jay-jay came to the area of the
parking lot. "Banquet Manager. Group Director. Executive Chef. Director of Services," read the yellow lines
on the macadam, reserving the ultimate honor in a
car-glutted world.
Next, he reconnoitered the loading platform. It didn't
smell nearly as nice as it did up front. He refused to pick
through the overflowing garbage cans. Wooden crates
were stacked up, and two heavy metal corrugated doors
sealed off any access to the kitchens.
Jay-jay chewed on his fingernail. "If you can't get in
on the ground level," he said, "then—"
Clambering up the crates, he grabbed the rain gutter
and hoisted himself onto the roof. The roof was flat over

the loading area, everywhere else it was peaked, with gray slate tiles that made it impossible to climb, even with sneakers.

Jay-jay quickly ruled out doing a Santa, all the chimneys were too narrow, some were even fake. Pebbles crunched under his shoes as he crept across the flat portion of the roof toward a glass skylight.

The moon broke free from the clouds, touching the trees and the Sheep Meadow that lay to the east. Jay-jay gazed at the silver scene for a transfixed moment and then pulled his eyes away. "To work." He inspected the panels of the skylight. They were constructed of heavy glass reinforced with mesh wire embedded into it.

"Even if you could break it, which I doubt, they'd discover it first thing and you'd never be able to get back again next week," he warned himself. "And that's not the plan."

Then Jay-jay spied a round—ventilator, it looked like. Made of aluminum. Standing three feet above the roof line. "Probably an exhaust for the kitchen," Jay-jay said eagerly.

There was a conical top on the ventilator, like a witch's hat. Two bolts held the hat in place. Jay-jay had his screwdriver out and working in a flash. He pocketed the bolts, eased the cone off the ventilator and looked down.

There was enough moonlight to see a large steel fan, about three feet in circumference, just below roof level. The kind of fan he'd seen in movies about old Southern plantations. But it was too dark to see what lay below it.

"Nothing ventured," Jay-jay said, and had one leg over the lip of the ventilator when the police car wheeled into the Tavern compound on its half-hour rounds.

Jay-jay yanked his foot free and dropped to the roof,

cursing himself for having forgotten. The beams of the car stabbed his way, reflecting off the plate glass windows of the restaurant.

The prowl car stopped just below where he was hiding. A cop got out of the car and checked the locks on the corrugated doors. At last Jay-jay heard the car door slam and it rolled away. He watched the headlights pick out a path across the Sheep Meadow.

Jay-jay forced himself to count to sixty before he got to his feet. One minute gone. If he was ever going to do it, it had to be now. "And you've got to be finished in less than twenty-nine minutes, and out of there or—" He drew his finger across his throat.

Twenty-one

Jay-jay hoisted himself into the ventilator and stood on the blades of the fan. Squeezing himself against the circumference of the air shaft, he eased himself through the grease-covered fan blades.

Chopped liver, if anybody flipped the switch, Jay-jay thought as he squirmed through. Ten pounds heavier and he wouldn't have made it. He still couldn't see what was below. Jay-jay hung from the edge of the fan blade and dropped. Onto a huge baffle plate and it sounded as if a giant gong had been struck.

He held his breath, waiting to see if anybody would come running. Another minute elapsed—precious time— before Jay-jay dared look over the edge of the nine-foot square metal plate.

He'd landed on what was really a fake ceiling. The

baffle plate helped draw the cooking smells and the heat to the ventilator shaft. It also prevented the city's dirt from falling directly into the kitchen.

The plate was suspended from the ceiling by four sturdy metal rods; about seven feet below the plate was the kitchen floor. The room looked even more enormous in the dark. The only light came from the red exit signs at either end of the cavernous space.

Like some kind of hell, Jay-jay thought, almost afraid to enter. The only thing more compelling than his fright was his hunger. Jay-jay eased himself over the edge and dropped, all the while thinking, Start planning ways to get out. Then he saw the answer. Good.

He started exploring. The kitchen complex was maybe sixty feet square with a lot of little rooms opening off it. Against the far wall were all sorts of cooking equipment. Giant vats, a grinder that looked like it could eat a cow, a salad maker and shredder. On another wall was a conveyor-belt dishwasher that was maybe forty feet long. The nearest wall had a bank of four cast-iron stoves and two deep fryers.

"I've got to find out where they've hidden the staples," Jay-jay breathed. "I've got to find out if there's a watchman on duty, though he'd be a deaf one not to have heard me. And what about the laser beam electric eye? Got to make sure I'm not caught in the middle."

But more important than any of these—"How come every time I go out on one of these forays I have to go to the bathroom?"

Through a double-arched doorway he went, into the dessert section. Freezers and cake shelves and a fantasy of spun sugar confections all under glass. They looked very expensive. "And sure to be missed," he groaned, resisting an urge to gobble one right then and there.

Jay-jay crept past the cashier's desk. A sign said:

Five Dollar Minimum After 9:00 P.M.

Jay-jay didn't go near the cash register. His cardinal rule was, only things he could use or eat. And green pieces of paper with black printing had nothing to do with that. "No," he whispered fiercely, "I *won't* let them make me a crook!"

Jay-jay entered a dingy corridor painted battleship gray and coated with cooking smells. Now he couldn't see anything. He banged his shin against the ice-maker, collided with a case of soda bottles. No choice; he'd have to light the precious tin of Sterno.

Gradually, his eyes grew accustomed to the tiny well of light. Overhead, a tangle of asbestos-covered pipes. On either side of the corridor, shelved cubicles stacked with supplies: Green and white linens, silverware, dishes and glasses, and all the thousand and one things that make up a restaurant.

And candles! Boxes full of thick utility candles. And charcoal briquettes. Quickly, Jay-jay transferred the light from the Sterno to a candle.

"See? If you hadn't risked lighting the Sterno you'd have never found the candles or the charcoal," he said, putting a box of both into his knapsack. "Sometimes, the only way is to take the risk."

Every time Jay-jay opened a door he expected Bluebeard or a watchman to grab him by the throat. He poked his way into a room full of circuit breakers and fuses and an emergency generator. For when Con

Edison fell down on the job. Like last summer, and the summer before, and all the summers to come.

Jay-jay's chest puffed slightly. He'd never have to depend on that. The breeze was his air conditioner, the sun his light and he felt more at peace with himself living according to the natural rhythms of the park.

Jay-jay reached the end of the corridor. He blew out the candle and Bluebeard through the swinging doors. Into a silver world he moved. Silver shone through the picture windows, silver shone off the white table cloths and sparkled from the silverware and silver lit up the white brick wall that moved in a semicircle around the main dining room.

A silver birch, enclosed in a rectangle of shatterproof glass, grew against the white wall, its branches spreading up over the gun-metal slate roof. The moon threw Jay-jay's shadow on the wall and he couldn't resist a moment of making himself a monster, a hero, bigger than life. Then an idea came to Jay-jay that he almost couldn't resist. He saw a table set for two, including china, silver, salt and pepper shakers, and wanted to sweep the place settings into his knapsack. "For when there's a celebration and I invite somebody up for dinner. Thanksgiving, maybe. You can't have Thanksgiving on paper plates."

Maybe I'll invite—what was her name? Deborah? Dolores? He couldn't remember. What about Mrs. Miller? he thought. She might have some trouble climbing the rope ladder, but she was a game old lady. And he'd help. I'll take the china and silver next time, Jay-jay decided. Can't carry everything, and tonight's for food.

Out of the dining room now and into a small lobby with beamed ceilings and a fireplace in the corner. At last!

The Men's Room. Beige wallpaper and beige tile floors and everything smelled of mothballs and relief.

The luminescent hands of the clock above the cigarette counter warned Jay-jay that he had seventeen minutes left. Through the ghostly private rooms he hurried, whose walls seemed to echo with the laughter of parties past and present, and into the banquet hall.

Mysteriously, Jay-jay was drawn to the center of the dance floor. His sneakers scuffed across the hardwood parquet. Jay-jay opened his mouth to hum himself an accompaniment, but only a croak came out. He turned and swayed, here where the fine ladies and their gentlemen had danced, while he had peeped in, eaten with envy.

Jay-jay stopped whirling and looked through the leaded windows to the silver expanse of his park. Suddenly, among all the beautiful furniture and the fine paintings, Jay-jay felt trapped. The walls seemed to close in on him and he realized that he was more scared of this room than he had ever been out of doors.

If being On-the-Outside-Looking-In had depressed him—well, being On-the-Inside-Looking-*Out* was a thousand times worse.

My way, true, you might get lonely sometimes, Jay-jay thought. But this way? Wow! This was a prison.

A grandfather clock in the corner chimed the quarter hour. Fifteen minutes before the cops made their rounds. Certain now that there were no hidden watchmen and that he had the freedom of the place, Jay-jay hurried back into the kitchen.

Once again, he lit the candle. "The food lockers first. Let's see, now. If the executive chef used his noodle he'd store the food close to the stoves."

Sure enough, off one corner was a narrow room and in

it, three wooden doors. The Meat Locker. The Vegetable Locker. And Staples.

None of the doors were locked. The meat locker was freezing! It was about twelve feet square, red tile floor, with floor-to-ceiling shelves lining three walls. Into the knapsack went a tin of ham, another of rolled turkey. There were dozens of these tins and he didn't think that they would be missed. On a serving platter lay slices of roast beef, left over from tonight's party. Jay-jay gorged himself on the meat while he piled other foods into the bag. He took only those things he thought would last the longest. Though the nights were getting real frosty, some days were still too warm for perishable stuff.

Into the vegetable locker next. This was almost identical to the meat locker, though not as cold, thank God. Two onions, two oranges, two apples, two melons. He put the melons back on the shelf. "Too heavy, and you'd better save space for things that are more nourishing," he said, munching on another piece of roast beef.

Though he would have preferred fresh vegetables, Jay-jay hadn't yet figured a way to cook them, so he took the canned goods. The final locker contained all the staples and that's where Jay-jay made the biggest haul. A can of powdered milk, powdered eggs, jar of honey, wheat germ, tin of powdered yeast. Then breadsticks, tins of sardines, salmon, chicken. He made sure he took a can opener, too.

He would have taken everything in sight, but the knapsack was so heavy that he had trouble lifting it. "Okay, don't be a hog, there's always next week." Jay-jay rearranged the cans on the shelves so that nothing looked out of place.

Jay-jay lugged his haul back to the baffle plate. Now to get out. He was about to start that operation when he heard a car pull up outside the building. For an instant he stood frozen, unable to move. Then the adrenalin shot through him.

"Don't panic. You've got it all planned." He blew out the candle. Nearby stood a counter on rollers, for stacking dishes, about six feet high. Working against time, Jay-jay rolled the counter under the edge of the baffle plate, hefted the knapsack onto the first shelf of the counter, and then climbed up on the shelf. He repeated the operation, moving his haul higher on the shelves until he reached the level of the false ceiling.

Jay-jay transferred the knapsack from the dish counter onto the baffle plate. He wedged the canvas bag up through the fan blades and rested it on one of the vanes. So far so good, he thought, though his heart was thumping wildly.

He started to chin himself up through the blades when he heard footsteps tramping down the corridor from the dining room and heading for the kitchen. Damn! You forgot the most important step! Jay-jay tiptoed back to the edge of the baffle plate and kicked the dish counter away. The counter rolled about a half dozen feet and came to a dead stop just as the two cops entered, outlined against the red glow of the exit sign.

Their flashlights swept around, slicing the darkness. Jay-jay hoisted himself up through the vanes of the fan and pressed himself hard against the cone of the ventilator.

Now Jay-jay couldn't see the cops because the false ceiling blocked his view, but he could hear them moving closer. Their searchlights roamed over the walls and the skylights, one of the policemen rolled a barrel over to the baffle; he got up on the keg and played his flashlight toward the ventilator.

Jay-jay could see the footprints he'd made on the dusty metal plate, but the cop's eye level wasn't that high.

"I could have sworn I saw a light in here," one cop said. The other grunted. After a final search of the kitchen and the lockers, they radioed the precinct on their walkie-talkie. "We have investigated the premises and there are no perpetrators in evidence. Ten-four."

When the police had finally gone, Jay-jay climbed out of the ventilator pipe and onto the roof. He screwed the conical cover back on and patted it. "See you next week." Heaving the knapsack onto his shoulders, he trudged across the roof and carefully climbed down the wooden crates to the loading platform.

As fast as he could under the weight, Jay-jay made for home.

Shadow was all ears as Jay-jay gave him a blow-by-blow description. "The secret is to plan as best you can, Shadow. But you've also got to stay loose so that if something comes up, you're cool enough to improvise. Got that?"

Shadow scratched his head.

Jay-jay said thoughtfully, "Now all we've got to do is keep that in mind for when Elmo shows up. Remember what I told you about the chickadee and that robbing grackle? Guerrilla tactics. So we've got to have a foolproof plan. What's more, we've got to rehearse it every day until it's letter perfect."

CONCLUSION

Twenty-two

November swept across the land, graying what was left of autumn until the park looked like a graveyard. Dead trees poked their fingers at a sullen sky. Jay-jay hurried home from a day's search for clothing, a heavy hooded parka bundled under his arm. Shadow, loping beside him, had found the prize at the football field.

Well, not exactly *found*, Jay-jay thought, bending to pet him. The coach had left it lying there, and in the excitement of the game Shadow had, well—

Jay-jay stopped at the secret hollow, uncovered the rope ladder and threw it up over the lowest limb of the oak. He climbed into the bower where the last of the parchment leaves somehow still clung. When Jay-jay reached the castle he let down a cardboard carton secured in a macramé rope cradle. As the carton reached the ground, Shadow hopped into the box and Jay-jay pulled him up.

Deep dusk and cold now, the wind had come up with approaching night.

Jay-jay rubbed his hands, glad to be in the warmth of the tent. The tent had turned out to be a snug home and much more than that. In the rare moments when he could relax from his chores, Jay-jay had taken to doodling on the canvas walls.

"Like the cave drawings I saw in the museum," he told Shadow, who was sitting patiently this twilight for his portrait. Shadow didn't seem to appreciate the likeness too much and turned away from it with a yawn.

"What's the matter?" Jay-jay asked. "It's got four legs and a tail, doesn't it?"

Jay-jay shrugged and moved on to his more ambitious project. On one whole wall of the tent he was in the process of drawing an area map of the park, including all the landmarks that he knew. Those few territories that he wasn't familiar with he marked "Unknown" in chalk.

"And just as soon as we explore that region, we'll erase the chalk marks," he told Shadow.

On the other wall of the tent, chipmunks, squirrels, the oak, the bench where he'd met Mrs. Miller, gulls and chickadees all had taken form under the growing sureness of his magic marker.

But then there was a dark shadowy figure whose face Jay-jay could never quite bring himself to draw.

When the light failed, Jay-jay put down his pen. For awhile, he watched the earth-toned colors of his domain grow somber. It was different than the fire-green of spring, or the riot of summer, or the blaze he had been surrounded with this autumn. This was quiet, more subtle, and in its own way, just as beautiful to Jay-jay.

On the verge of opening another tin of hash for a cold supper, Jay-jay decided to treat himself and Shadow to a big spread.

"Why not, Shadow, we've earned it." Anyway, Jay-jay thought, it's got to be around Thanksgiving time. "Tonight *feels* like a celebration, hot meal and all."

Days before, Jay-jay had lugged a large concave stone up to the platform and converted it into a hearth. It stood just outside the tent. Following his successful raid on the tavern, Jay-jay had gone back and liberated cooking utensils, place settings, and of course, more food. He had built a shelf one branch higher in the oak and stored all the household equipment there.

Jay-jay reached up for a tin of boned turkey and opened it. Soon turkey slices were sizzling in the skillet along with candied yams. The savory odor made Jay-jay salivate as he shelled hazelnuts for an after-dinner treat. Shadow circled the hearthstone, sniffing and wagging his tail.

So engrossed with his chores was Jay-jay that he would not have been aware of the new presence if an awakened screech owl, and Shadow, hadn't given the alarm. Jay-jay leaned over the battlements and looked own.

His heart contracted into a tight fist. Elmo stood at the base of the oak, drawn by the cooking odors and the flicker of red in the tree. Elmo might never have found him, so well had the tree camouflaged his house, but the smells had given Jay-jay away.

Elmo had spent the week scouring the area, drawing a circle tighter and tighter around the northern reaches of the park. He knew it was the only place wild enough to hide in, but somehow the kid had always eluded him. But this time he had him cornered, and Elmo's blood began to pound with the sureness of the kill.

Elmo circled the trunk, looking for a way to climb up. He strained and tugged—how the hell had the little bastard managed it? It was breaking his back just to get a foothold.

For a fleeting second, Jay-jay thought of dropping the burning coals down on Elmo, like Greek fire. But that would risk setting the entire forest ablaze. Instead, Jay-jay carried out the plan he'd devised for just such an emergency. Moving fast, he stuffed the rope ladder into his parka, piled his belongings into the knapsack, struck the tent. Climbing high into the tree, Jay-jay tied the bag onto a branch too weak for Elmo to reach. Two days before, Jay-jay had tested this limb and knew it would not support the weight of anybody much heavier than himself.

So carefully had Jay-jay organized and practiced all this that he completed it before Elmo had figured out how to get up into the tree. When Jay-jay climbed back down to the platform he was ready to defend his home. Shadow was ready too, his milk teeth bared to the oncoming invader.

Meanwhile, Elmo had finally gained the first branch. Hand over hand Elmo climbed, until he reached the level of the wooden platform.

"Into the elevator, Shadow," Jay-jay ordered, prepared to lower him to the ground. But Shadow had other ideas. As Elmo's hand came over the platform, Shadow dashed forward and nipped him. Elmo snatched his hand back.

After a moment, his hand appeared over the edge again, but this time, the switchblade was open in his fist. Jay-jay tried to grab Shadow, but the dog squirmed from his grasp, growling and snapping at Elmo.

"Now you're going to get it," Elmo muttered, his breath coming in short gasps. Elmo had ditched the methadone program; his last fix had left him feeling fuzzy and a little weak. "But still strong enough to take care of you," Elmo spat.

I can't fight him off here, Jay-jay thought, his eyes traveling upward to the thinner branches. Stay out of his reach, that's what I've go to do. Lure him away from the castle.

Once more Shadow went for Elmo's fingers. Elmo yowled and dropped the knife. It fell, disappearing into the darkness. Elmo grabbed the pup's tail and before Jay-jay could stop him he hurled Shadow off the platform.

Jay-jay screamed. Shadow's fall was broken by a network of branches, but he landed with a thud. Jay-jay peered desperately at the ground. It was too dark to see.

"Shadow? Shadow!" But there was no sound. "You killed him!" Jay-jay shouted.

Elmo had his knee over the edge of the flooring. Jay-jay backed off to the other side and started to climb down the branches, just as Elmo gained the platform.

"You slippery little son-of-a-bitch!" Elmo yelled and leaped to follow Jay-jay.

Jay-jay knew the tree by heart. In the darkness his feet found purchase on the limbs. Elmo was not so fortunate and twice he slipped, enough to slow him down. Jay-jay reached the lowest branch, looped his ladder over the limb and slid down, knot to knot, dropping to the ground just as Elmo reached that branch. But before Elmo could use the ladder Jay-jay yanked on one length of the rope and it fell to the ground, leaving Elmo stranded on the limb.

"Shadow, where are you?" Jay-jay called urgently. Still no answer. "Oh, God, no," Jay-jay moaned. Then a ray of reason penetrated his despair. Even if I did find Shadow, what could I do? If Elmo gets ahold of me, both me and Shadow will be goners.

Feeling like an idiot because he was marooned on the limb, Elmo jumped. He landed hard, knocking the wind out of him.

Jay-jay stopped his search for Shadow and beat it down the hill. Here too, Jay-jay knew all the rocks and pitfalls. They seemed to signal their presence and he avoided them.

Elmo, breath partially regained, tumbled after, tripping on exposed roots, falling over moldy branches. At the base of the Great Hill Jay-jay fled across the sounding planks of the footbridge. The park lay in total darkness now save for the tiny islands of light from the sparse lamps along the paths.

Jay-jay kept to the underbrush. He heard Elmo crashing behind him, but he had enough of a lead so that he might really lose him. Though I don't know what good that will do, Jay-jay thought. Elmo will come back the next day, or the next, to get me.

Jay-jay made his way along the rocky shoreline of the waterfall, keeping low. The white froth of water raced alongside him.

Panting for breath, Jay-jay sought refuge in the small dank cave at the entrance to the tunnel. Instantly he regretted his decision, recognizing it as a trap. Jay-jay dashed out of the cave and tore through the echoing blackness of the tunnel. Emerging from the other end, he left the path and climbed into the bramble bushes dotting the hill.

He lay still, hearing his heart thud against the ground and in his ears. Jay-jay listened hard . . . nothing . . . maybe Elmo had given up? No, there was the crack of twigs. Elmo passed below him. Just when Jay-jay thought he was safe a hand reached into the bushes and yanked him to his feet.

They fought on the hillock, Elmo holding him easily at arms' length, Jay-jay kicking and straining to break free. Methodically, Elmo slapped him. Jay-jay's head jerked to one side, then the other. The blows got harder. Blood fountained from Jay-jay's nose. Elmo's fingers closed into a fist and Jay-jay felt the knuckles hit his cheekbone.

Jay-jay sagged to his knees. Another punch knocked out a loose tooth; with a distant awareness Jay-jay realized that was the last of his baby teeth. Elmo was punching him around the head now. A knee jabbed into Jay-jay's stomach, knocking the breath out of him. He felt the warm trickle of blood in his mouth and then he collapsed.

Elmo let Jay-jay drop. He kicked him in the side. "That's for stealing my rowboat." The kick hadn't hurt Jay-jay too much, but the second one did and Jay-jay knew that if Elmo kept it up—

Elmo flipped Jay-jay onto his back. Elmo straddled his chest, knees digging into Jay-jay's arms. Jay-jay stared up at the pale glinting eyes. Fingers were around his throat, pressing tighter until his breath strangled and his eyes bulged. All at once the pressure relaxed, Elmo . looked at him, a toying smile on his lips.

Jay-jay's fingers scrabbled in the dirt searching for anything he could use as a weapon. His hand closed around a short, thick stick. He swung it up hard just as Elmo sensed his move. Elmo tried to dodge the thrust but it caught him in the Adam's apple. Elmo rolled off Jay-jay, his throat working in dry heaves.

Jay-jay scrambled away, cutting across the plain that adjoined the Loch. A last-chance idea was shaping in his head. The Police Station at Eighty-fifth Street. Elmo was insane! And he couldn't handle that alone. Jay-jay prayed that a patrol car would come cruising by. But they were never around when you needed them!

When he reached the Ninety-seventh Street Transverse, Jay-jay crossed the overpass and swung east around the shore of the Reservoir. He ran on through the darkness, slowing down to a walk when he had no breath left, then loping again when he thought he heard something in the bush. Past the Woodsman's Gate at Ninety-fifth Street, past the Engineer's Gate at 90th, around the Reservoir and had just gotten to the Gate House when Elmo caught up with him.

The Police Station was only about three hundred feet away! But Elmo, taking a short cut through a stand of evergreens had cut him off. Jay-jay opened his mouth to yell but his breathless scream came out a croak. Jay-jay veered off to the south, running aimlessly now. Elmo, wheezing and holding his throat kept his pace steady, taking a perverse pleasure in letting the boy run until he dropped from exhaustion.

The dark presence of the Metropolitan Museum moved by and soon Jay-jay came to the Seventy-ninth Street Transverse. There was the Cedar Hill construction all lit up with spotlights, *Tyrannosaurus rex* craning its red neck over the fence. "Maybe they've still got that guard inside," Jay-jay whimpered, and, dragging his way to the front, pounded on the double doors. Before anybody could respond, Elmo was on him again.

The chase took them around the wooden fence to the curving stone cliff that rose from the sunken roadway of the Transverse. There were no spotlights on this side of the excavation, only the intermittent flashes of head-lights from cars careening around the curves twenty-five feet below.

Jay-jay climbed up on the retaining wall, balancing himself as he'd done the day he'd first reconnoitered the construction camp. His head still reeled; blood had dried in his mouth and nose and there was a buzzing in his ears. He felt light-headed and heavy in the limbs as he walked the ledge. Slowly at first, then increasing his pace as he remembered how.

He came to the break in the wall where the native rock jutted out over the roadway. Only about three feet, Jay-jay thought, then there's the black cherry tree. Remember how you did it before!

Pressing his body against the rock, he tried not to look down to where the cars charged along, intent on their own breakneck goals. Headlights cut through the darkness and threw the two disjointed shadows onto the night.

Jay-jay felt Elmo's fingers close around the sleeve of his parka. With the last of his strength he tore free and rounded the outcropping of rock. He heard a cry and whirled to see Elmo lose his footing. Elmo's windmilling hands caught the retaining wall and he hung there, over the roadway.

Freedom lay ahead of Jay-jay. More than anything, he

wanted Elmo to get what he deserved. But could he just let him hang there to die? And then Jay-jay discovered that Elmo's way was not his way.

Jay-jay inched back along the wall. Below, streams of cars continued to whiz by. Elmo's fingers whitened as he clutched the stone railing, his feet kicking against the granite blocks fighting for a foothold. Jay-jay grabbed Elmo's wrist. They fought there, winning an inch and losing it in a fearful symmetry.

"Hang on!" Jay-jay cried, feeling Elmo's fingers slipping from his grasp. Elmo looked at Jay-jay for one hopeless second and then he fell to the roadway, bouncing off the hood of one speeding car and tossed under the wheels of the next.

Brakes screeched, horns blared. Elmo paid no mind. His eyes were blank and unseeing in the headlight beams.

In the grip of massive shock, Jay-jay stared down. He did not dare believe what he saw, but the snarled traffic was a reality he could not deny. Then his hands moved with a will of their own and lifted the medal from around his neck. He pressed the chain and medallion in his fist, then opened his fingers and let the medal fall down to Elmo's body.

Then Jay-jay sagged against the rock and fainted.

Twenty-three

Toward dawn, Jay-jay slowly regained consciousness, becoming aware first of his aching body. He opened his eyes but only one worked, his left eye was swollen shut. A low hum just below him made him turn and look—the Transverse—and it all came back to him.

Traffic was rolling again; the police cars and the ambulance had long since gone.

"Elmo's dead," Jay-jay whispered, not quite believing it.

Bowed and beaten, Jay-jay made his way back to the oak. He searched the bushes and found Shadow lying in a clump of arrowwood. Jay-jay started to cry. For Shadow, for Elmo, for all the things that would never be. He lifted Shadow to carry him to a burial place—

"You're still warm!" Jay-jay shouted. He pressed his ear to the dog's chest and heard the almost imperceptible heartbeat. Shadow's left paw hung awkwardly and Jay-jay cradled it.

"Alive, alive," Jay-jay repeated over and over as he carried Shadow up into the oak. "Don't you worry, my Shadow, we did it once before," he said urgently. "Got you healthy, and we'll do it again."

Depressed, elated, for the next few days Jay-jay swung perilously between the two moods. On a downer whenever he remembered the sickening thud as Elmo's body hit the road; really flying when Shadow responded to his care and got strong enough to lap up some milk and powdered eggs. Using the bandages he'd taken from the school health office and a couple of sticks of wood, Jay-jay had improvised a splint for Shadow's broken leg. In the reflecting mirror of the Loch, Jay-jay was able to see that his own bruises were healing, his purple eye had turned to an iridescent green.

In his quiet times Jay-jay thought a lot. He knew that Elmo's death would stay with him forever. But somehow Jay-jay also recognized that must not stop him from living. He had chosen a course for his life and that was as important as anybody's death.

Then there came a day when the sky turned dark, a slate color that looked wet and the bleakness made Jay-jay shiver with the feeling that something was about to happen, something that he had dreaded these many weeks.

It happened at dusk. The snow fell then and the white wind howled all about. Jay-jay battened down the tent till not a draft entered. Then he made a small charcoal fire on his stone hearth and continued with his chores.

"Snow means tracks," Jay-jay explained to Shadow, "so we've got to make snowshoes out of rags and paper," and he showed the dog his handiwork.

The snow continued to fall until Jay-jay was ready for bed. He crept into his sleeping bag, Shadow snuggled beside him. Jay-jay opened a flap on the tent and looked out. Still falling, steadier and softer, and in spite of all his apprehensions, Jay-jay felt a certain peace. The warmth of his own body filled the peaked space and he yawned.

"A resting time for the land, maybe," he said drowsily. "For the tree. For us, too."

Through his half-closed lids Jay-jay watched his domain transformed into something pale and blue and pure.

So quietly had the falling blanket muffled all sound that Jay-jay slept late the next morning. When he got up and stepped outside he saw a landscape so dazzling that it took his breath away.

"Shadow, come look!" Jay-jay called.

Shadow wiggled out of the sleeping bag, then, using his splint as a crutch, hopped to the tent opening.

The boughs were weighted with snow, boulders and ravines were softened, and the wind drift had sculpted unearthly shapes all over the land.

Jay-jay shook his head slowly. "The thing that I've been most scared of all these months—? Turns out to be the most beautiful sight I've ever seen. And look!" he cried, pointing at the platform and tarpaulin completely covered by the snowfall. "It's even camouflaged our castle! Nobody can see us!"

Breakfast was easier today than normal, he didn't have to climb down to the brook for water, he just scooped it from the platform in handfuls. Shadow was just starting on dessert when he looked up and made an attempt to growl, the hair on his back bristling into a ridge.

Jay-jay cupped his eyes with his hands and scanned the territory. Something was working its way slowly down the path, something that looked a little like—a honey bear? It was bundled up in galoshes and a brown turban and a fake fur coat. Then Jay-jay recognized Mrs. Miller.

While she had been drinking her morning tea, Mrs. Miller had listened to a news special about violence in the park . . . a young boy killed there a few days before. Frantically, she had called the radio station but they couldn't give her any further information. Her phone call to the police station had led to three different departments before she was cut off. For ten minutes she had paced the apartment, watching the snowstorm. The doctor had advised her to take it easy for another week. But she could stand it no longer and had dressed and hurried to the park.

Mrs. Miller stopped at her bench. She brushed the snow off the slats, but all she saw were the remnants of the old messages. Her shoulders slumped. Then she lifted her head and called across the snowdrifts to the stand of trees marching up the Great Hill.

"Little boy? Where are you? Are you still here? I'm all better now, thank you very much. Little boy, you must be hungry, you must be cold. Come home with me."

The moaning wind was her only answer and Mrs. Miller felt the tears well to her eyes.

Jay-jay pondered her offer as the dazzling crystals continued to fall on his kingdom. He touched his nose to Shadow's cold muzzle. "It's your decision too, Shadow, but better let me explain everything so you can decide.

"See, Shadow, the best part is coming up. This cold is the hardest. But soon everything will bust out again. New flowers and fire grass and green, green leaves, and it will all grow brighter and better and stronger."

Shadow looked at him with his enormous trusting eyes.

Jay-jay continued, "Concerts at night, rock and pop, high brow and low brow, take your pick, and dandelion salads and Shakespeare and happenings and no cars on Sundays, we'll have all that to look forward to. You'll see, Shadow, the city will come out of its sleep, people will wake up and come back to their park. And that will be the best time. All that's going to happen, Shadow, I promise."

In answer, Shadow sneezed.

"Little boy—" Mrs. Miller began but her voice faltered. She brushed the snow that had covered her shoulders, then took out a handkerchief and wiped her eyes.

"But wait a minute," Jay-jay said anxiously. "Why is Mrs. Miller crying? I guess she thinks maybe that something is wrong. Shadow, you stay here. I'll be right back. I've got to tell her we're okay."

As Mrs. Miller turned to retrace her steps, she saw a small figure floating down from the trees. Her mouth fell open and she watched, as though it were a vision from on high.

And then he was standing before her. Looking younger than she'd remembered. Maybe because he was in a parka that came down to his ankles. But his cheeks were flushed and he didn't look wild-eyed or gaunt like that first time.

"I'm so glad to see you," Mrs. Miller began. "You see, I heard on the radio—" She told Jay-jay about the news broadcast.

Jay-jay bit his lip. "That was Elmo, the guy who mugged you? He was chasing me and he—" Jay-jay broke off.

Mrs. Miller clapped her hand to her cheek. "Terrible, terrible," she whispered. "That I never wished on him."

"Me either," Jay-jay murmured.

Then Mrs. Miller saw the bruises on the boy's face and realized the ordeal he must have gone through. For her. "But you're all right?" she asked.

"Fine."

"Maybe we should tell the police?" Mrs. Miller said.

Jay-jay took a step back.

"Wait! Only so that somebody should know," she added hastily.

"God knows," Jay-jay said.

Mrs. Miller nodded slowly. She posed her next question with great care lest the boy fade away as mysteriously as he had appeared. "I was wondering . . . if you would like to come home with me."

"Gee, thanks a lot," Jay-jay said, "But I've got my own place. Besides, I've got this dog, Shadow? And he's pretty sick. I just couldn't desert him."

"No, of course not. But your dog can come and stay with us too," Mrs. Miller said. "We'll find what to feed him. And you know what else? We can call in a veterinarian? Only for consultation," she added quickly, seeing the guarded look in Jay-jay's eyes.

"I'd have to ask Shadow about that," Jay-jay said dubiously. "I look out for him, you know."

"But who looks out for you? Is somebody feeding you?"

Jay-jay shook his head. "Only myself. Good things, too. Why don't you come to dinner sometimes?"

"I'd like that very much," Mrs. Miller said, completely mystified. She waited a beat. "You look like a smart boy," she said. "So you know that this is only the beginning of winter. It will get cold, very cold. Enough for you to freeze without ever realizing it, and then it will be too late. For your dog, too."

She saw the flicker of doubt cloud his eyes. "You don't have to make up your mind today, or even tomorrow," Mrs. Miller said as they continued along the path. "Decide whenever you want."

"I don't think I'm finished yet with what I've got to do here," Jay-jay said soberly.

"What?" she asked softly.

He shrugged "I'm not sure myself. But someday, maybe soon, we can be roommates."

"I hope so," Mrs. Miller said. "Because I like you. I like you very much." Resisting an urge to sweep the ragged boy into her arms and smother him with kisses, Mrs. Miller contented herself with reaching out and patting him on the shoulder. "Here, I knitted this scarf for you."

They continued up the path until they reached the Boy's Gate. Jay-jay held out his hand. Mrs. Miller took off her glove and she and Jay-jay shook hands very formally.

"Good-bye then," she said. "You'll think about what I told you? Even if you just want to do it for the coldest nights, you're always welcome."

Jay-jay nodded. "Oh, thanks for the scarf. It's great."

Mrs. Miller started across the avenue and turned. "I'll see you tomorrow?"

"See you tomorrow," Jay-jay called back, waving.

Making sure to stay in Mrs. Miller's footprints, Jay-jay very carefully made his way back to his oak. He pondered everything that she had said.

"Of course, I could live here forever," Jay-jay said to himself. "But it might be better for Shadow, seeing as how he's sick and all. I'll just have to talk it over with him."

He scooped up a handful of snow, packed it tight and threw it up at the branches of a pine tree. An avalanche of snow engulfed him. Then he stuck his tongue out as far as he could, reveling in the burning-cold sensation as he caught the snowflakes.

His whole realm turned into a rainbow as Jay-jay looked through the muted prisms of the snowflakes that clung to his lashes. And it seemed to him that he had the best of everything he'd ever dreamed of. His freedom. Somebody who liked him. Jay-jay did a one-step, then a two, and in his cracked, changing voice, he started to sing.

Acknowledgments

Special thanks to Peggy Brooks for her invaluable help in editing this manuscript. Grateful acknowledgment is also made to Antoinette Marie Bunker, Isabel Leighton Bunker, and Robert Thixton of Pinder Lane Productions for all their encouragement and support; to C. Frank Ross and George S. B. Morgan, who accompanied me on some of the more dangerous explorations of Central Park; to Henry Hope Reed and Sophia Duckworth, whose book *Central Park* provided me with valuable source material; and to Constance and Stephen Spahn and the students at the Dwight School, who allowed me to sit in on their classes and observe them at work and at play.

HB3E

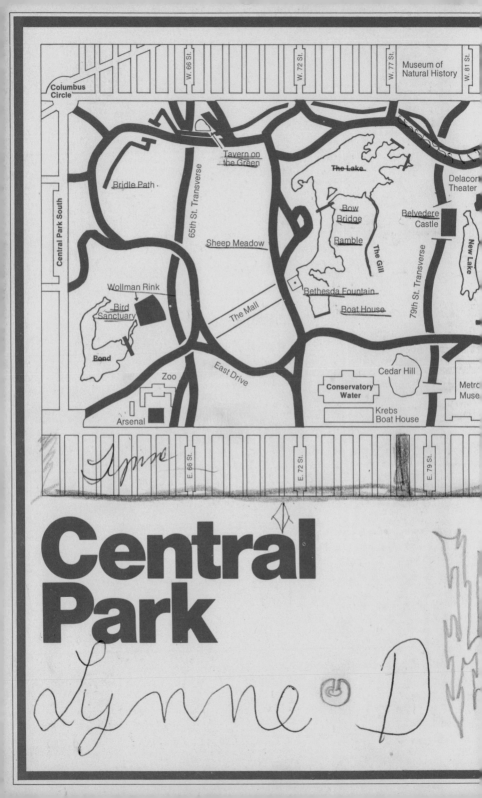